She crossed a continent to find a new life, a new world . . . and maybe, a new love. She discovered that life in the big city wasn't always all it was cracked up to be—and that sometimes, it was even more. She's found a terrific friend, a not-so-terrific roommate, and a *very* confusing relationship with her Resident Adviser. For Felicity Porter, the first year of college is a real adventure—and now you can join in the fun with this behind-the-scenes guide, packed with facts, photos, a *Felicity* quiz, and more!

FELICITY AND FRIENDS

felicity
AND
friends

KRISTIN SPARKS

BERKLEY BOULEVARD BOOKS, NEW YORK

This book was not authorized, prepared, approved, licensed, or endorsed by any entity involved in creating or producing the *Felicity* television series.

FELICITY AND FRIENDS

A Berkley Boulevard Book / published by arrangement with Aladnam Enterprises, Inc.

PRINTING HISTORY
Berkley Boulevard edition / February 1999

The Penguin Putnam Inc. World Wide Web site address is
http://www.penguinputnam.com

ISBN: 0-425-17089-6

BERKLEY BOULEVARD
Berkley Boulevard Books are published by The Berkley Publishing
Group, a member of Penguin Putnam Inc., 375 Hudson Street,
New York, New York 10014.
BERKLEY BOULEVARD and its logo
are trademarks belonging to Berkley Publishing Corporation.

PRINTED IN THE UNITED STATES OF AMERICA

10 9 8 7 6 5 4 3 2 1

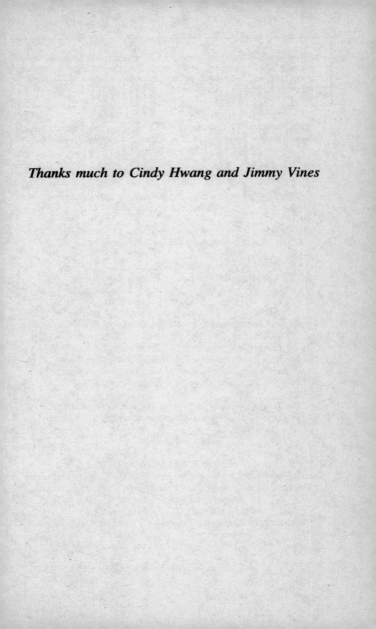

Thanks much to Cindy Hwang and Jimmy Vines

Contents

CHAPTER ONE
Welcome to *Felicity*   1

CHAPTER TWO
The Keri Facts   5

CHAPTER THREE
The Pure Felicity of *Felicity*   27

CHAPTER FOUR
Keri—Now   37

CHAPTER FIVE
Keri's Squeeze   47

CHAPTER SIX
Not Just Another Scott   51

CHAPTER SEVEN
Amy's Aim   61

CHAPTER EIGHT
Kicking Back with Amy Jo   73

CHAPTER NINE
Greet Scott! 79

CHAPTER TEN
That Tangi Tang 89

CHAPTER ELEVEN
The Pink Guy 97

CHAPTER TWELVE
The Show and Its Creators 101

CHAPTER THIRTEEN
The Producers 113

CHAPTER FOURTEEN
But What Are People *Saying*? 125

CHAPTER FIFTEEN
Sally 135

CHAPTER SIXTEEN
Scandal! 139

CHAPTER SEVENTEEN
Touring the Web with *Felicity* 145

CHAPTER EIGHTEEN
The Best Bet for
Felicity Fan Action 157

CHAPTER NINETEEN
Show by Show 161

Contents

CHAPTER TWENTY
Music   169

CHAPTER TWENTY-ONE
Felicity Forever   175

CHAPTER TWENTY-TWO
Felicity and College—
True or False?   177

Welcome to *Felicity*

Ever done anything really brave and life-changing? Something that may seem normal to others, but is actually very scary to you?

Probably one of the scariest, most exciting, and incredible things you'll ever do—or have already done—is to leave home to go to college in another state.

The much-praised new WB series *Felicity* is about just that. Felicity, the title character, in fact, changes her life with a vengeance. She decides not to go to nearby Stanford University, as her parents have planned. Instead, she heads all the way across the country to New York City—and all to be close to a boy she's idolized for years.

But *Felicity* is about more than that.

"College," says Keri Russell, who plays Felicity, in the January 1999 issue of *YM* magazine, "is being out of your comfort zone. I think that's ultimately what our show is about: coming to a new place and being able to reinvent yourself!''

On Tuesday, September 29, 1998, at 9:00 P.M., The WB, a brave and innovative new network, debuted a series not quite like anything ever seen before on American TV. A show called *Felicity*.

The show won the highest Nielsen ratings that any WB show had ever gotten before.

Why?

Well, certainly coming after the wildly popular *Buffy the Vampire Slayer* didn't hurt.

However, there was more to it than that. *Felicity* and its stars—Scott Foley as Noel, Amy Jo Johnson as Julie, Scott Speedman as Ben, and Keri Russell as Felicity (especially Keri)—had been getting a great buzz of excitement from the people who'd seen the pilot for the show—the reviewers, the advertisers, television-station folk.

These strikingly attractive and personable actors began showing up on covers and in articles all over the North American continent. Keri Russell even made the cover of *Seventeen*, long before the debut date.

Not even the awesome *Dawson's Creek* cast had caused this kind of stir early in the year, when Kevin Williamson's daring, sassy, and absorbing show debuted on The WB.

How did *Felicity* manage to arouse such excitement? And how has it maintained that enthusiasm and transformed it into something new—something real, immediate, and now?

Well, I'm going to tell you that right here in this hot little book. I'm going to tell you about the creators, J. J. Abrams and Matt Reeves, and how they took an idea born in the exotic South Seas, an idea that was first intended as a feature film, and made it into a TV show. I'm going to tell you about how they took a theme—the thrill and fear of making important choices in a young life—and turned it into such an absorbing series. I'm going to tell you about what the critics said, about the scandals and rumors, the trials and tribulations, and the real-life drama behind the fictional drama.

As the producers point out, though, there would be no *Felicity* without the incredible, gorgeous, yet sweet and fun actors who have put such life and vitality into this show.

Where are they from? What have they done before? What would it be like if you sat down with them and talked to them? What would it be like if you knew them?

You're going to love them even more when you find out, I promise!

t w o

The Keri Facts

Can you imagine being Felicity Porter's best friend?

A nice thought, huh?

She's sweet and human and dear. She's, like, so funny sometimes, like when she's playing Boggle.

Most of all, she's someone you can trust. You just know you can. I mean, she makes mistakes just like you do, but she's honest and apologizes, right?

Now, if you were Felicity's best friend and you were in New Mexico like her friend Sally, maybe you'd talk into your tape recorder and trade your most intimate thoughts and secrets that way. You'd get to hear all about Ben and Noel and the goings-on at the University of New York and the Pink

Ranger . . . ooops, I mean Julie. And that grumpy chemistry professor.

But if you were Felicity Porter's best friend, it would probably be a lot more fun if you were there, smack in the middle of Manhattan with her. You'd get to go to Broadway shows. You'd meet the most fascinating array of people imaginable. But most of all you'd have a wonderful pal . . .

Someone you could trust!

You'd hang in the coffee shop, sipping sodas or whatever and know . . . just know . . . that this was just the best time of your life . . .

Ever!

Yes, that's the feeling you get, whether you're male or female, about this character. She's just so shy, yet sweet and cuddly. She's cute, but she doesn't wear makeup or get flashy and she's got these deep eyes and deep thoughts . . .

You could just sit in that coffee shop and look at those hazel eyes amid all that coffee-shop background chatter and just laugh and talk for hours . . .

That's Felicity Porter, age eighteen.

But you get the feeling that it's Keri Russell, age twenty-two, as well, who plays the title character on The WB network show *Felicity*.

Let's get a little closer to Keri, shall we?

TAKE A NUMBER, PLEASE

Can you believe it?
Keri almost didn't get the role of Felicity.

In the script for the pilot episode, the character was supposed to be a wallflower.

Problem? Well, Keri Russell is no wallflower and she's certainly not a drab nothing. In fact, she's SO not a nothing in the looks department that she got her start as a model. So what's she doing in the role of Felicity Porter, a shy NoCal gal who nests in bulky sweaters and jeans and thinks she has to fly from West Coast to East Coast to get a shot at a guy?

The creators, Matt Reeves and J. J. Abrams, thought she might be TOO beautiful for the part.

When Keri walked into that crowded room to audition for the much-coveted role, they weren't sure.

"She was the first person who read the part as funny," J. J. Abrams reports in *Seventeen*.

That's what sold them on Keri.

Fortunately also, Keri had the L.A. smarts to dress down for the role even while auditioning, and her acting ability is such that although the camera does not lie, it was clear that this was one attractive person who was able to *act* mousy.

She's been doing a great job of that ever since, but still, often, she's gorgeous in a really gentle way.

Maybe that's Keri Russell's secret . . . beyond her obvious acting abilities . . .

CAN KERI KISS?

Can you imagine being Felicity Porter's boy-friend?

She was pretty much a loner, you know, back in high school in Palo Alto. She probably wore glasses and baggy clothes and she spent a lot of time in study hall.

True, she talked in class and was pretty much a straight-A student, but when she got out she didn't seem to hang with the popular kids. Yes, she had friends . . .

You could have asked her out. And suppose you had, and you got along. And you were at the movies or something, sitting beside all that hair and sweetness, with her perfume near you and that tub of popcorn and giant cup of Coke . . .

It's a boring part of the movie, and you lean over, and those wonderful lips are so near and . . .

Oh dear! You spilled your soda . . .

No. It doesn't take long to see that Felicity spilled hers on you.

She's just that kind of gal.

That's what makes her so different and special and real.

DOWN-TO-EARTH WITH KERI

"Felicity is simultaneously reckless and fearful," Keri Russell reports in *New York* magazine.

"But she's also really intelligent and that saves her ass a lot of time."

Keri!

Such language!

Still, it shows that Keri's a down-to-earth sort, and she's certainly intelligent. Although her acting career has so far kept her out of college herself, she got straight A's in high school.

Besides, you can see it in her eyes.

Keri attended Highlands Ranch High School in Colorado, but the Boulder State is not where she's from.

Yep. Like Felicity, she is a member of that Beach Boys song.

Keri Russell is a California girl. She was born in Fountain Valley, to be exact, just a few miles from the Pacific Ocean beach. Fountain Valley is just below Los Angeles, in Orange County. If you were in Disneyland and decided you needed to surf and headed straight for the waves, you'd pass right by Fountain Valley.

Keri sounds like a form of the popular Irish name Kerry, but in fact that wasn't where it came from. She had a grandfather whose name was Kermit. Kermit the Baby was clearly a bit too much for the Russell family, so they dubbed the new tyke "Keri."

If you must know exact dates for astrological purposes or whatever, Keri was born March 23, 1976. Her father is David Russell and her mother's name is Stephanie. An older brother, Todd, was already talking by then (Todd was born in 1972) and in 1979 she got a younger sister, Julie.

But no, Keri didn't immediately get whisked away into baby-food commercials when she was born. In fact, her show-business career took a rather roundabout route.

She and her family spent some time in Dallas, Texas, and then moved to Mesa, Arizona. There in Mesa, at Keno Junior High School, Keri not only entered her teen years—she discovered talent and love.

She loved dancing.

Keri adored all kinds of dancing and worked hard at them all. She worked at styles as diverse as ballet and street dancing all the way to jazz dance.

"[I learned] everything," Keri told a chat group at the Universal Studios WebPage. "I had scholarships at studios, which meant I had to take seventeen classes a week. So that pretty much covered everything."

Hard work enabled her to join the Mesa Stars Dance and Drill Team. Her excellence won those scholarships mentioned in the quote above, allowing her to study in fine programs. The Stars Dance and Drill Team toured the country, doing numbers at National Basketball Association games and National Football League game halftimes. The group also took her to Sydney, Australia, where they participated in the World Fair Expo '88.

But did the people who saw her dance ever think she would be such a success?

Stars director Bobbi Rogers did.

''She's the kind of person you believe would do it,'' Rogers told Jaime Rose of the *Arizona Republic* regarding her feelings about her former student becoming a star.

In fact, Keri has been quoted in the press as saying that she really isn't an actress. Perhaps she is being modest, because her acting is just fine in *Felicity*.

However, there's always the chance that Keri still thinks of herself, first and foremost, as a dancer.

After the next bit, maybe you'll understand why.

WHO'S THE LEADER OF THE CLUB?

Remember back in the good ol' days of TV, when there was real entertainment on the air? Back when Disney produced this great afternoon TV show named after their most famous cartoon character. Yes, this show was just chockablock with great variety. Singing and Dancing . . . Spin and Marty . . . The Hardy Boys . . . Roy and Jimmy . . . Annette Funicello . . .

Wait a minute. Wrong generation.

Fast forward.

When the Disney Channel on cable became a success, it was natural that they'd think about doing a new version of one of their most popular shows . . .

Yes, the one with Annette and Company.

The Mickey Mouse Club.

You know. M-I-C-K-E-Y M-O-U-S-E.

Only of course they had to update it and film it in color. In the days of yore, the show had been associated with Disneyland. It seemed appropriate that *The All-New Mickey Mouse Club* should be associated with the New Disney Kingdom.

You guessed it. Walt Disney World.

And you might also guess where this is headed: Keri became a Mouseketeer.

It happened like this:

Keri's father worked for Nissan (the car company, of course). He was moved by his company to Denver, Colorado. In the big city, Keri attended Highlands Ranch High School.

"I SO was her [Felicity] in high school," Keri noted in the November 1998 issue of *Detour* magazine. "I moved to Colorado from Arizona when I was thirteen, and that's a bad time to uproot. So I had one best girlfriend. I didn't fit in any group. I kind of voyeuristically watched high school pass by, which is complete Felicity."

Keri's smile at least looked like good material to photographers. Soon she was modeling in Denver, but honestly didn't care for it. If saying cheese wasn't Keri's cup of Cheddar tea, nonetheless it did open opportunities to her. And remember, she still loved to dance.

Boy, wouldn't you love to have saved up old tapes of Ed McMahon's *Talent Search*? No? Well, if you had, and you just happened to have the right one, you'd be able to see Keri make her first appearance on television.

It was because of this appearance that talent scouts from the Disney Company saw Keri.

First, she auditioned and got a part in the film *Honey, I Blew Up the Kids*.

Then she got the Mouse ears.

You want to hear about Keri as a Mouseketeer? You'll have to wait a moment.

Let's talk about Keri in *Honey, I Blew Up the Kids*.

THE INCREDIBLE SHRINKING KERI

From the first time you see Keri Russell in this Disney movie, you know she is star material.

Keri is booming down a water slide. She's age fifteen and she's in a bikini that suits her well, true—yes, and those curls are flying and that button nose and perfect chin are there . . .

But look at those eyes and that mouth—they're open wide and they're simply sparkling with life and verve. There's no way that even George Lucas's Industrial Light and Magic could artificially reproduce the sparkle and sorcery they exhibit.

There's absolutely no question in the viewers' minds, the moment they lay eyes on Keri, why the fifteen-year-old Nick (reduced to a tiny size with his sister in *Honey, I Shrunk the Kids*, to which this film is the sequel) has a crush on her.

Yes, true, in the next glimpse the director, Randal Kleiser, gives us is Keri and that bikini. It's overkill, though. Keri's got that something . . . That IT factor that moviemakers and theatergoers and television watchers have talked about since the days of Clara Bow in the silent movies.

What is IT? Well, it's sex appeal, sure . . . But it's more than that . . . We've all known what it's like to be with a vibrant, amazingly alive person. Only often that doesn't translate well into television or film. Cinema and video, after all, are just records of light. There has to be an interaction between a person and the camera that creates something special.

That's IT.

That's Keri.

In *Honey, I Blew Up the Kids*, Keri plays Mandy—a bouncy baby-sitter who gets drawn into the plot not only by Nick's crush, but by Dr. Wayne Zsalinski's request that she watch two-year-old son Adam for a few hours. Wayne (Rick Moranis) is an inventor. Wayne was the guy who, in the first movie, invented a ray gun that reduced his other kids to the size of bugs for an incredible and funny adventure. In this film, though, Wayne's working for a large corporation trying to figure out how to make things BIGGER. As you might guess, baby Adam accidently gets zapped by the new BIGGER ray gun. He grows and grows until he's a huge kid. Giggling, he runs amok in Las Vegas.

It's no wonder that Keri has had fans ever since this movie. Although this was not exactly a Meryl Streep role, she did put spunk and sass into her acting. She's in a large part of the movie, interacting with a lot of special effects (like how about being tempted by a giant M&M?) and she's perky and vivacious and fun.

But that wasn't the end of Keri's connection with Disney!

SHE'S GOT EARS

There was nothing mousy about this mouseketeer!

From 1991 to 1993, Keri Russell appeared on *The Mickey Mouse Club* on the Disney Channel.

The Mickey Mouse Club is filmed in the Disney Studios part of the Disney World complex, and Keri had to move to the Sunshine State to work on the show.

She sang and she danced and she learned to drive.

That's right.

She learned to drive in the Magic Kingdom, she told a magazine.

Maybe it was her instinct to return to the sun that brought her to Florida. In any case, there was more than just oranges that thrived those years in our southernmost state.

"I love it," Keri said in *The Disney Channel's Mickey Mouse Club Special Collector's Magazine* in 1991. "I'm having the time of my life and it is the best learning experience."

She apparently got along well with the other Mouseketeers. "As long as I'm with people I like, I don't have to go somewhere to have fun."

Although the show is gone, this *Mickey Mouse Club* still has fans. There are still WebPages that remember it—and Keri's work with the Club.

She sang and danced, of course.

And she learned to act with help from an acting instructor named Gary Spatz.

CUDDLY AND DUDLEY, ETC.

In *Daddy's Girls*, a 1994 CBS series that didn't last very long, Keri stretched her range.

"[Dudley] Moore plays the daddy in this show's title, father to three daughters, the most amusing of whom is sixteen-year-old Phoebe (Keri Russell), a charming dim-bulb dating the amiably stupid Sear

(Phil Buckman),'' reported Ken Tucker in his September 30, 1994, review of the show in *Entertainment Weekly*.

Keri in a sitcom?

Well, we have to face it. Keri cannot only do just about anything, she already has.

Like *Spin and Marty* in the original *Mickey Mouse Club*, the latest version had a serial as well called *Emerald Cove*, in which Keri played Andrea McKinley.

She's appeared in commercials for Jack in the Box, JCPenney, Sears, and Lee jeans.

She's been in episodes of *Boy Meets World* and *Married with Children*.

So why not a sitcom?

Keri got much higher marks than the series star, Dudley Moore, however. And since not a huge number of people tuned in, the show was canceled.

Keri Russell took this in stride and moved on to greener pastures.

MALIBU HILLS ZIP CODE

In 1996, Aaron Spelling tried to see if lightning would strike twice.

The famous TV producer took the formula of his famous hit *Beverly Hills 90210* and created something in the same mold, but with enough of a different tweak and spin to make it feel fresh. To keep the Tori Spelling tradition up, Spelling cast his son, Randy Spelling, in this one.

However, he also had the smarts to cast Keri Russell.

When she got this role, "I think that I first told my Mom, 'Hi! I totally got the part,' " Keri told *Bop* magazine in a 1996 interview.

In *Malibu Shores,* Keri plays Chloe, daughter to a rich family who live in the famous Malibu. It seems that Chloe falls hard for Zack, a working-class sort from the San Fernando Valley. Zack is played by Tony Lucca.

This is a significant fact for Keri fans.

Tony Lucca is not only an actor, but an individual with great musical talent. These talents got Tony a job in the cast of *The Mickey Mouse Club* about the same time as Keri.

Apparently they not only sang and danced together. (More on this later, promise!)

People magazine announced that the show was "colorful, lustrous junk" but didn't like Keri and Tony too much.

Anyway, *Malibu Shores* failed to make the grade, lasting only eight episodes.

However, it still has fans.

One particularly fun WebPage devoted to this show is the *Amish Guy's Malibu Shores WebPage,* believe it or not.

You can find it at:

http://wesjen.simplenet.com/mshores/

Who says Aaron Spelling fans don't have a sense of humor?

A VERY LONG WEEK

A film based on a title of a Beatles song?

Sounds great!

I'd like to see it.

Unfortunately, Keri's movie *Eight Days a Week* apparently has appeared only at film festivals and is still awaiting a wider release.

Still, it really sounds like something!

Apparently, it's a teen comedy that's a bit racy, a little bit on the tarter side of *Dawson's Creek*.

Written and directed by newcomer Michael Davis, the film is decidedly low-budget, but has perked up some interest at the film fests, even earning an award at one of them.

The film concerns a guy named Peter who has a huge crush on the beautiful Erica.

Can we guess who plays Erica?

Peter and Erica have just graduated from high school. The story concerns the summer before college. Peter is desperate. Keri—I mean, Erica—has paid no attention to him. So he camps out in her front yard, like Romeo before Juliet's balcony, entreating her to return his love.

Apparently, Keri gets to wear a lot of sexy outfits

as she walks past her suitor on her way to see her handsome but nasty boyfriend Nick, and the film is supposed to be fun.

''Russell is a decidedly alluring Lolita . . .'' reports Todd McCarthy in *Variety*, January 20, 1997.

Prediction: Thanks to the attention that Keri Russell is getting, thanks to *Felicity,* this film should be available soon.

Lots of folks want to see more of Keri!

A TWISTY SHADE OF *SCREAM*

Keri Russell in a horror movie?

Keri Russell running around in a skimpy outfit, chased by a maniac with a knife?

Well, not quite.

Dead Man's Curve (a.k.a. *The Curve*), like *Felicity,* happens on a college campus but features intrigue of a decidedly deadlier sort than what happens every week at the University of New York.

Filmed in the Baltimore area, *Dead Man's Curve* concerns guys who think that university policy not only allows the roommates of a student who kills himself to have the rest of a semester off, but gives them a 4.0 grade-point average for that session.

The good guy in this is Chris. The bad guys are his roommates Tim and Rand. No reason to give away the plot dynamics here. Let's just point out that Keri Russell plays Chris's girlfriend, Emma, and she get's involved with the decidedly dark doings.

According to Dennis Harvey of *Variety*, "*Dead Man's Curve* cynically paints campus life as a place where the apparent most popular major is advanced sociopathy."

There are twist endings and more twist endings, which make one wonder if maybe Keri might not be a villain in this film. (Say it's not so!) The director and writer, Dan Rosen, also wrote the black comedy *The Last Supper*.

It should be in movie theaters soon.

And probably in video stores sooner than the creators would like!

AN IRISH LASS

"Being in Ireland alone was wonderful," Keri Russell told James Brady of *Parade* magazine. "When I was not shooting I went to Trinity [College in Dublin] and just sat on the steps thinking, 'I could drop out and just go to college and become a real person.'"

The film that Keri was speaking about is *Mad About Mambo*, which will probably be Keri's best movie role so far. It was from the set of this movie (which is coproduced by Gabriel Byrne's production company) that Keri flew to New York for her *Seventeen* magazine cover shoot and interview, both of which turned out extremely well despite a major case of jet lag.

Mad About Mambo was shot entirely in Dublin,

Ireland, with its Sheriff's Street doubling as Falls Road in Belfast, Northern Ireland—appropriate since the film is supposed to take place in that troubled city.

Keri Russell plays a Northern Irish girl learning Latin dance in special dance classes—who meets the film's hero, Danny Mitchell, while he is learning the mambo for unusual reasons. Unlike his Belfast school friend Mickey, who wants to be a fashion designer so he can meet beautiful models, Danny isn't into dancing to meet members of the opposite sex. And he's not like his friend Gary who wants to be a magician so he can meet beautiful magician's assistants. No, Danny has come to the conclusion that if he can dance like a South American—with the same pizzazz, footwork, and dazzling moves—then he can master soccer like South American soccer players.

Naturally, he falls for Keri's character.

Of course, Keri's looks and her dancing ability qualified her for the role.

But there was more to the mix.

When asked by Juan Morales of *Detour* magazine about Keri's denial of being an actress, famous Irish actor Gabriel Byrne was quick to disagree.

''Keri's modesty is admirable, but the objective reality is that she is a very talented actress and totally convincing as a young girl from Belfast. Her performance has 'star' written all over it.''

Mad About Mambo, a romantic comedy, looks

to be a totally different role for Keri and one that *Felicity* fans will want to catch.

Can't wait to hear Keri speaking in a Northern Irish accent!

BITS AND PIECES

As that article in the November '98 *Detour* pointed out, Keri Russell became famous like a character in Hemingway's *The Sun Also Rises*: "gradually and then suddenly."

Keri Russell, in the past seven years or so, has seldom been out of work.

Well, what else has she done?

Remember that Bon Jovi video "Always" a few years ago? Yep, that was Keri in that video.

In 1996, she made two guest appearances on *Married with Children.*

In 1996, she appeared in the NBC movie called *The Baby-sitter's Seduction* as Michelle Winston, an eighteen-year-old girl who has an affair with a man (Stephen Collins) who might have killed his wife.

Also in 1996, Keri appeared in a TV movie based on the famous Shirley Jackson story "The Lottery" as a girl who falls for a stranger in a town with sinister secrets.

The year 1997 found Keri on an episode of *7th Heaven*, this time not playing sweet and adorable. In fact she plays a character named Camille, a rebellious teen whom one of the show's characters meets in detention hall and decides to accompany to a wild fraternity party. (Felicity in a toga? Anyone have a tape?)

Also in 1997, Keri starred in *When Innocence Was Lost* on the Lifetime Channel.

DEATH FOR KERI

"It was my first death scene," Keri said on the *Universal Chat Log*. "At first I thought it would be really corny, but I really liked the way it was done. A lot of it was done in slow motion, so it was definitely foreign. I wasn't used to doing it, but I enjoyed it."

Keri was speaking about her role as Claire, the girlfriend of the main character, Connor, of the series *Roar*. She'd tried out for the role with Shaun Cassidy, a former teen idol himself and now a television creator and producer. She got the part immediately.

Roar was an unusual and exciting adventure series taking place in the magical times of the Dark Ages.

Keri had hoped to make guest appearances on the show after her death as a "Spirit."

Alas, the show was not renewed.

WORKING

Keri has been so busy working all these years that she never had a chance to actually do what Felicity does:

Go to college.

College is still an option for the future, though, Keri noted in a recent interview.

Let's take a look at how this delightful ingenue with smarts but limited education got the job, and what she thinks about the character and the show.

t H R E E

The Pure Felicity of
Felicity

KERI IN CHARACTER

In *Webster's Seventh New Collegiate Dictionary*, the word "felicity" is defined thusly:

1. a. The quality or state of being happy. Especially great happiness.
1. b. An instance of happiness.
2. Something that causes happiness.
3. A pleasing faculty esp. in art or language.
4. An apt expression.

Perfect, no?

The character of Felicity causes us happiness.

Of course, she's quite a bit more complex than that. This is one of the appealing aspects of Felicity Porter.

Oh yes! Porter. What does that mean in the same dictionary. Let's see . . .

1. One who carries burdens.

Well, of course it means like luggage, but nonetheless Matt Reeves and J. J. Abrams clearly had reference books ready when they were figuring out their heroine's name.

Felicity Porter is happy, yes, but she carries burdens.

For one thing, she takes everything very seriously. She's a deep thinker. You can tell this by her conversations with her friend Sally via the tape recorder. Everything is just so deep and important.

Why else would she fly off the handle and sign up to attend a New York university to be around Ben?

More importantly, how else would she realize that this incredible gaffe, this mistaking a flirtatious signing of her yearbook, would send her exactly where she should be?

Only a deep thinker would have realized this, and only a deep thinker would realize the opportunities that living in Manhattan and attending an East Coast university had to offer.

There are similarities here between Felicity before U of NY . . .

. . . And Keri Russell before *Felicity*.

In a conversation with *Teen People* available

only on America Online, Keri revealed that before she'd discovered that an actress was being sought for this new TV show, she'd pretty much been adrift, rolling along in her career, doing just about everything.

The role of Felicity was, she says, "my first conscious choice" of a character to play.

Why was this?

Well, think back all the way to Keri's first movie role. That would be Mandy in *Honey, I Blew Up the Kids*.

Apparently, the qualities of Mandy stayed with Keri through her whole career.

"I was there to be the cute girl and kiss the guy," Keri told *Detour* magazine. "Literally that was my job. I can't tell you how many times I've been paid just to kiss the main guy."

This was pretty much the sort of role that Keri got most of her career, and she became upset at the way girls were represented. Although not critical of Aaron Spelling Productions, she feels that *Malibu Shores* suffered from this as well and that nothing resembled reality.

The character of Felicity, though, she was able to define to *Teen People Online* in one word:

"Real."

Keri's disappointment with teen-babe-busses-boy syndrome led her to accept a project that was not so hot, but had the virtue of being set in New Orleans. Keri thought that this would be an opportunity to see more of the world, and have new experiences and a chance to work on her personal life.

However, then, the script for *Felicity* came in.

She ditched the New Orleans gig and instructed her agents to get her into the audition for the role.

What was it about the role of Felicity Porter that made Keri Russell act this way?

Of course it was true that plenty of actresses wanted the role. When parts become available for TV shows, it's not like producers and casting agents have to look very hard. Nonetheless, in retrospect, when you look at Felicity as a character, and you think about Keri, you can kind of understand what she's talking about.

Felicity Porter is the kind of girl who gets straight A's in high school but doesn't necessarily speak up much in class. She's always alert and aware, but she's quiet. Real quiet, like she's nervous about saying anything . . .

You've seen her type.

Maybe you ARE her type.

Things are just so overwhelming . . . Everything that's going on . . . School, family, job, vacations, whatever . . . just is so amazing but so MUCH . . . But whenever you reach out to someone you don't really know to talk about things, words tumble out, get stuck together, and nothing quite works out right.

So you just shut up.

If you're like Felicity, you're quiet, yes . . . And

also quite attractive, but you don't necessary FEEL attractive.

If you're like Felicity, you really need deep, close friends . . . You need to talk to them and be close and near to them . . .

If you're like Felicity, though, there's something else that goes on.

J. J. Abrams, cocreator and executive producer of the show, probably says it best.

"I remember saying to [Keri] one day, 'You do these scenes so deeply, and yet they don't seem to be exactly who you are.' And she told me, 'Felicity sort of says all of the things that I think but I'm too afraid to say,' " he told the *Los Angeles Times* for their September 27, 1998, Calendar section.

That's it! That's the thing about Felicity.

She's impulsive.

It's her impulsiveness that sends her sprawling away from her parents' plans for her premed career at Stanford and into New York City.

And though Felicity is quiet and sweet, she's also capable of expressing lots of other emotions.

Like, who can forget that scene with Noel? It's set in the middle of a fancy restaurant meal during a "maybe date" with dorm adviser Noel after an awkward kiss from him spoils a Boggle game. Noel spills the news that he already has a girlfriend at another college. What's her reaction?

She blows up at him.

It's a great scene, and excruciatingly embarrassing for vulnerable, sweet-faced Noel, as Felicity, wondering if maybe Noel, not Ben, might be the right guy for her, tears into him for hiding this fact.

The astonishing thing is that we've never seen Felicity get this mad before. But it's entirely in character because it's an impulsive, even funny fit of rage and indignity.

And it feels so, well, real!

REAL REALITY

As you may recall from our look at her twenty-two-year biography-in-the-making, Keri's high-school experience was very much like Felicity's.

This was one of the reasons that Keri liked this character so much, and why she told her agents to beg for her to get a shot at the role.

Basically, despite her looks and intelligence, Felicity is a bit of an oddball. Like many other students, she doesn't quite fit into things and never quite has. What makes life even more awkward for poor Felicity is that at the University of New York, she's a duck out of water, and an odd duck at that. Raised and pampered in an affluent area of sunny California, she is suddenly thrust into scary, gritty New York City. It's not even as though she's going from softball to hardball. Poor Felicity is going from JACKS to hardball!

"I think and feel everything Felicity says," Keri told *TV Guide* in their special "Young Hollywood'' issue. "She's just a caricature of me. I make all those lame faces, just not always to strangers. I have a little censor in my brain that says, 'Don't do that.' She doesn't have that yet, and that's great. I wish I had more of her in me.''

And those sweaters!

"I can just imagine someone from California buying all sorts of big alpaca-wool numbers to come East!'' reports Lise of girlson.com.

Lise also notes, quite perceptively, that although she's gorgeous, Keri as Felicity also looks like a real-life college student. Lise reports that she will continue tuning in to *Felicity* because the show can deal with teen and twenties issues in a noncondescending way.

"Part of the show's expansive appeal, I think,'' says John Carman in his review of the first episode in the September 29 issue of the *San Francisco Chronicle*, "is that [Keri] Russell doesn't look like the college student of the 1990s. She looks like any time. She looks like then, she looks like now, she looks like all the time.''

Keri pretty much says it all about her character in the November issue of *Twist*:

"I love that she can be a basket case and smart and funny at the same time. I love that she doesn't wear any makeup and puts her hair back in a ponytail and wears big baggy clothes and you know, not swimsuits. Girls don't always have perfect makeup and sweaters and fake boobs.''

* * *

Keri Russell was determined the win the part.

When she arrived to try out, Keri had washed off all her makeup, bunned her hair, and wore a baggy sweater and scuffed jeans.

Despite this disguise, the producers were struck by her looks and thought she'd be a no-go. However, Keri read a lot of humor into the part, and won their hearts.

In the *L.A. Times* Calendar section for September 29, Matt Reeves is quoted as saying, "We read a lot of people, but we just didn't have the person who took the role and made it her own. The show is so emotional, if you didn't relate to the character the way that you do, I don't think it would have any value. It's not just that she plays Felicity. There is no Felicity without Keri Russell."

"Keri made shooting comfortable and easy," Scott Foley asserts in his interview with The WB's *Dawson's Creek* page. "I saw the pilot and she is amazing. She blows me out of the water. I think it's because of her that the show does well. You want to know her. She makes you want to know Felicity. And she makes you care. America is going to fall in love with Keri Russell."

So how did Keri Russell get the role of Felicity?

Well, her looks helped, certainly—even if she had to work extra hard to play them down.

The more you look at the facts, though, the more

you get the picture of a talented young actress who not only saw an opportunity for a role of a lifetime in *Felicity* . . .

She saw much of herself . . .

And much of others.

She got the role.

The rest is history . . .

. . . and the future . . .

f o u r

Keri—Now

THE PAWS THAT REFRESH

What's it like to be Keri's cat?

It must be nice and purry to be able to curl up and watch TV with such a pleasant person. So affectionate, too. Probably lots of stroking and soft words and scratches in—ooh!—just the right places. With a long history of cat owning, the Russell family can assure you that Keri knows how to pet a cat properly.

And on what she makes as an actress, you can bet that Keri Russell's feline is not chowing down on generic cat food! Kitty Gourmet, more like!

Keri's cat, for the record, is named Nala.

Let's ask Nala.

"What's it really like to be Keri's cat?" says Nala. "Lonely! She's gone so much!"

Just kidding!

Make no mistake about it, from Keri's place in Pacific Palisades, where she lives the single life, Nala may have a beautiful view of the ocean or of Steven Spielberg or Sylvester Stallone's magnificent homes . . . But Keri is gone a great deal of the time. Chances are that her boyfriend took care of Nala when Keri was in Ireland (boyfriends do serve some purposes), but now that Keri is back and deep in *Felicity*, Nala is . . .

Well, then again, who can say? Maybe Keri can take Nala to the set and keep her in her trailer sometimes. Things could be harder for a cat.

Certainly, Nala couldn't have a nicer person for an owner!

So the answer to "What's it like to be Nala?" we must conclude . . .

Great!

KERI'S LIFE

If Nala indeed accompanies Keri to the set of *Felicity*, then she has to get up awfully early in the morning . . . and go to bed very early as well.

"My life is so boring," Keri told *Seventeen* magazine. "I'm in bed by ten-thirty every night!"

Exhausted, probably.

The really big secret Hollywood TV stars have is how hard they work. Oh, sure, it's not like driving a truck all day, but it's still work, and it takes a certain pluck and ability to make it through. Getting up at five in the morning is not uncommon for an actress who has to report at six-thirty for makeup. Work on the set often starts as early as eight—and fourteen-to-sixteen-hour days are not uncommon.

Stamina.

That's one quality Keri must have.

Of course, being a dancer, she has to have stamina.

Just how early Keri gets up is her own private business, but chances are, it's way too early.

How can we guess that Keri is nice and honest? Well, certainly she comes across that way in interviews ... But then, she's supposed to ... Still, there's an authenticity there.

In the *Felicity* computer mailing list, though, there was recent proof. A woman wrote saying that she'd met Keri at a dance competition about eight or nine years ago and has been a fan ever since, Keri was such a good dancer and so nice.

Nice and genuine. That's the feeling you get about Keri. It's so easy to imagine going for coffee with her at one of the cool hangouts in Los Angeles (maybe to watch her boyfriend play guitar or to see Amy Jo Johnson's band). Keri would drink latte with whole milk and probably really enjoy getting out and relaxing and hoping no one would recognize her.

You also get the feeling that her family is very

supportive of her and her talent . . . and always has been.

As early as *The Mickey Mouse Club,* she was talking about her family.

"They don't care what I do, which I like a lot," she told *The Mickey Mouse Club Special Collector's Magazine.* She also gets "the brother-sister treatment, which keeps me honest."

Her older brother, Todd, has a cat named Oreo. (Colored black and white, perhaps?) Younger sister, you'll be glad to know, has a feline companion as well. That cat's name is Groovy. (In seventies-style multicolor?)

Keri's parents, David and Stephanie, are still together, which Keri thinks is wonderful. They live in Dallas, Texas, but they certainly keep in touch.

INTIMATE DETAILS

Keri has a nickname!

Care Bear.

As Care Bears go back to the eighties, she must have gotten it then, although whether it was her parents or her friends who gave it to her must remain a deep, bright mystery.

If you've had a hard time telling what color Keri's eyes are from her many pictures in magazines and on the Web, it's because they can change color between green and hazel.

Apparently her eyes aren't all that changes color,

though. Those amazing Botticelli curls were orig-
inally brunette, but have dipped into blond from
time to time.

Her favorite color is green.

When she commutes back and forth between the
set where *Felicity* is shot in Culver City, she drives
a Nissan pickup (green?) and may well be listening
to her favorite singers, Tori Amos, Vince Gill,
Sarah McLachlan, or Bryan Adams, on the sound
system. (She's said in interviews that her favorite
car's a Jeep, so maybe she owns one by now.) But
chances are she's listening to All News KNX, 1070
("Traffic and Weather Together!") in order to
dodge the traffic snarls on Route 405 in that Nissan
pickup or Jeep.

Pacific Palisades, her pad's location, is actually
closer to Malibu Beach than to Culver City, but
Keri doesn't seem to be much into swimming or
surfing. No, her favorite sports are basketball and
baseball. (She especially enjoys watching Grant
Hill play basketball.)

If she were to slip into some shoes to play either
of those sports, they'd be size five. We knew you'd
want to know that!

Oh. And what does she do to make her hair so
beautiful?

"I don't do anything with it," she told a fan at
a Universal Web site chat. "It does its own thing.
I have no control."

Now, supposing you and Keri finished your lattes and still had some free time . . .

What would you do?

Well, you would go shopping, maybe. (Although not for Versace, because Keri's not into fancy clothes like that.) She does like to go to the beach sometimes, so that's a possibility. Maybe Rollerblading? She's good at that, and it's good exercise.

Oh yes, and movies! Keri loves to go see movies. And if the movie is with Ethan Hawke—she's there!

If her family is in town, Keri would have another favorite thing to do: barbecue with them.

Apparently, it's a long-standing tradition in the Russell family and it seems fitting that they should do it in Southern California, where backyard barbecuing got its start. And to drink with the charbroiled goodies? A Virgin piña colada would probably be her choice. (That means a piña colada without alcohol.)

If it rained on the Russell family picnic and you needed something quick to eat before that Ethan Hawke movie, Keri would choose Carl's Jr.

Carl's? Why?

Maybe because drip happens . . .

And if it happens to Felicity, you can bet it happens to Keri.

NICE . . . AND MORE

Certainly Keri would like to grow as an actress and continue enjoying success.

Who doesn't want to be successful?

However, there's one thing that Keri doesn't want to be.

A "star."

When Bruce Newman of the *Los Angeles Times* used the S-word, Keri stuck out her tongue and made a face.

"Even that word," she said. "Oooh . . . ugh."

In the same article, she did a very Felicity kind of thing by blurting out something critical about one of the current TV goddesses and then regretting her remark. However, the reporter was enough of a gentleman not to print the remark—and point out how much Keri's character was like her TV counterpart's, Felicity.

(Who was Keri talking about? Probably not Sarah Michelle Gellar of *Buffy the Vampire Slayer* fame, since that actress is also handled by Keri's manager, Joannie Burstein.)

Keri's remark was apparently about the girl's career, not the girl herself, who Keri thought was very nice. However, Keri got all flustered, Felicity style, afterward . . .

Nonetheless, this is one person with opinions!

When asked by Newman about the current fashion and popularity of horror thrillers, for instance, she responded:

"I hope this whole teen horror-film genre ends, actually, I think these producers don't get that kids are smarter than that."

Keri is pretty much overwhelmed by all the attention she's been receiving. You get the feeling that she truly is considering going to a real college, just to escape from it all.

Probably the biggest shock was the *Seventeen* spread. She has a hard time even talking about it. When the *L.A. Times* reporter showed it to her, she just rolled her eyes: "That's where I get all *my* information about the world!"

When *Harper's Bazaar* asked her what would happen if *Felicity* flopped, she said, "I could move to Colorado and become a ranch hand. You never know."

However, she seemed a lot more exhausted when James Brady of *Parade* caught up with her while she was in New York doing location shooting for *Felicity*.

What would happen if there were only thirteen episodes of the show?

"I'd go to Hawaii," said Keri, "and do nothing. Absolutely nothing!"

In *YM*, Jeanne Wolf asked her what she kept in her dressing room, to help calm her down with all the work she has to do.

"Candles and pictures," Keri responded. "I take a lot of black and white pictures and I've been using a lot of the photos I have in my dressing room on the set—in [Felicity's] room. Pictures of my goddaughter and people I love."

Well, since those interviews, *Felicity* has been picked up for the full season by The WB. Nine more shows, at the very least, so Keri will have a lot more work to do.

And of course, even if *Felicity* only lasts one season (impossible!), while the show's been getting great reviews, Keri's been getting super reviews.

"[Keri] Russell never seems to make a false move or hit a wrong note," Tom Shales of *The Washington Post* praises. "She's a glory in a nicely manageable TV-size way."

After making a few critical knocks at the show, Robert Bianco of *USA Today* says, "Any qualms I have about the show don't extend to [Keri] Russell, who seems headed for TV stardom and beyond. She has the rare ability to grab the camera, to make you focus on her, even when someone else is talking."

Not fond of *Felicity*'s earnestness, the *New York Times* nonetheless points out that "With her clear-eyed gaze and Pre-Raphaelite hair, [Keri] Russell is immensely likable yet down to earth."

And it looks like Keri will be working hard for a while!

SIGNIFICANT OTHERS

Although *Felicity* is certainly a show that doesn't quite have the smooch factor of *Dawson's Creek* (seems like all those characters do when they're not having crises or wisecracking or making hip cultural allusions is make out), it certainly has a set of vibrant and electric and sexy actors who surely must be attracted to each other on the set.

Right?

Well, not really.

For one thing, Keri's got a longtime boyfriend, Tony.

For another, the cast members only just met!

Fortunately, they get along well.

"We hang out extracurricularly," Keri told *Teen People*. "Amy Jo plays guitar and sings at some local places and we all go check it out. We've hung out together at my place too. It's been cool."

You can bet that Nala liked it, too.

But a boyfriend, you say?

Tony?

Tell all!

five

Keri's Squeeze

LONGTIME COMPANION

When asked if she has a boyfriend now, Keri Russell is happy to respond "Yes."

His name is Tony Lucca.

Besides acknowledging Tony as her steady, Keri also calls him her best friend.

He also sounds like one heck of a terrific guy!

It's pretty easy for Keri fans to figure out where she met Tony. He costarred with her on *The Mickey Mouse Club*. And although theirs has apparently been an on-again, off-again relationship (she's been reported to be dating Joey Lawrence, for instance), right now it seems very much on.

You can also see how they stayed in touch over the years, even if they weren't dating. For one thing, Tony Lucca was Keri's costar in *Malibu*

Shores as her upper-class character's working-class flame.

Presumably, if you have tapes of that show, you can even see some of the chemistry between them.

Tony's a dark, good-looking guy with short hair and nice eyes. A real heartthrob, certainly. But you get the feeling that there's more between him and Keri than just physical attraction. It looks as though they have the kind of relationship, in fact, that Felicity longs for.

Although Tony's an actor, his main love is music, which was how he got the job on *The Mickey Mouse Club*.

Just like Keri, Tony is twenty-two years old and he lives close to her in the Palisades area of Los Angeles.

Tony was born and raised in a large family. He decided to be a musician when he was seven years old, and was influenced very much by his parents' favorites, Crosby, Stills and Nash and Joni Mitchell. Presently, he cites his musical influences as jazz greats John Coltrane and Miles Davis, as well as pop musicians such as Sting, Ben Harper, Counting Crows, Lenny Kravitz, and Jeff Buckley.

Keri has called Tony's music "soul-folk."

Whatever it is, it certainly is excellent.

If you can't get to Los Angeles to hear Tony Lucca play at any number of clubs there, you can catch some of his excellent music at the Web site devoted to him, the *Tony Lucca Homepage* http://www.luccamusic.com.

There's some clever text here written by Tony, and you can see his picture. You can hear samples of his music if you have the right kind of Web software. It's really good stuff. The CD is called *So Satisfied*.

If you don't have a computer, though, you write to Lucca Music to get the CD. (A self-addressed stamped envelope would be the best bet for a fast response.)

LUCCA MUSIC
15332 Antioch St., #130
Pacific Palisades, CA 90272

Tony has just gone into the studio to record a second album. He's been gigging with friends in different groups here and there as well as playing solo.

There's not a whole heck of a lot of information about Tony out there, but there's some fascinating notes to his fans on the Lucca Music WebPage. He doesn't say a single word about Keri, and Keri really doesn't talk much about Tony.

However, Keri has said one fascinating thing about her very first kiss.

"I was sixteen," she told Julie Trelling of *YM*.

"My first kiss that counts was with a boy who had never kissed anyone before. It was good because we were both bad. I still see him. He's so cute that I'm always like, That was a good choice."

Knowing what we know, you gotta think:

Was that Tony?

Not Just Another Scott

BEN OUT OF SHAPE

In a show filled with interesting characters, perhaps the most surprising—and subtly drawn—is that of Ben Covington.

Ben is the Hunk.

Some articles about *Felicity* have called the character the Stud.

Ben Covington is the perfect male, admired from afar by a dowdy soul. He is the dreamboat straight out of *Tigerbeat* magazine that Felicity would like to take a cruise on.

That beautiful blond hair. Those deep, sparkling eyes. That strong chin. Those strong legs as he competes in track and field. But perhaps what Felicity detects beneath the Adonis good looks is a poetic, gentle, thoughtful soul.

Ben is certainly soft-spoken enough, with a nice smile and good manners. It's easy to understand how a shy girl like Felicity would have a crush on him all the way through high school.

But Ben Covington is not quite the guy Felicity thinks he is . . . He's got all those elements, sure . . . But there are other sides to him.

Nonetheless, Felicity has been dreaming of him for years, and has followed him to New York City all the way from Palo Alto, California.

"You have to remember," J. J. Abrams pointed on *E! Online*, "that Ben is someone she's had feelings for for many years. Giving up Ben is like giving up a bad habit. But Ben is going to show sides to his character that will put him in a little bit of a bad light."

Yeah. Like inviting Felicity to the Halloween party and then making out with the Pink Ranger!

Yeah. Like failing to make the university track team and then lying to Felicity by saying that he'd decided not to try out.

Still, the thing is that not only is Ben basically a nice guy, he's still very gorgeous and thoughtful . . . Plus, as you get to know Ben Covington, you realize why he is the way he is, and the past he's grappling with.

Ben is the reason that Felicity is in New York— but why is Ben in New York? Basically, it's because, we learn, he had a rough family life. His father is an alcoholic. His is not the perfect all-

American life. His is a young life all too common in America.

That's why Ben is becoming such an interesting and well-rounded character.

That's why we still care about him, despite the rotten things he does to Felicity sometimes.

"I think [the producers] had trouble filling the role," Scott Speedman told the *Calgary Sun* about his part. "I think most actors fell into the trap of playing him as the tough guy, not being a real guy with heart. That's what I did want to show."

THE ALL-AMERICAN CANADIAN

Scott Speedman feels as though the character of Ben is a lot like he was when he was nineteen . . . Searching for himself and making mistakes.

Although Scott was born in London in 1976, he was raised in Toronto.

His youth was dominated by athletics.

In 1992, he was on the Canadian Junior National Swim Team, doing those pool laps like nobody's business. Scott did so well, in fact, that he made the Olympic trials. There, his performance was excellent enough to give him hopes of heading to the next Olympic games.

Unfortunately for sports and luckily for *Felicity,* he hurt his neck, which took him out of swimming entirely.

Scott always had a strong interest in acting, however.

When he heard that Warner Brothers was in his hometown of Toronto, casting for actors for their new film *Batman Forever,* he thought that he would make a darned good Robin.

On Canadian television at the time, there was a show called *Speaker's Corner,* where everyday citizens could stand before a camera and speak their minds. (Based on the Speaker's Corner tradition of London's Hyde Park, where all sorts of people are permitted to get up and make speeches.)

Scott thought it was a good place to tell the world why he'd make a good Robin, the Boy Wonder.

"To be honest, I don't know what I was thinking when I did that," he told the *Calgary Sun.* "I was going to a high school with a big drama program, but I was in the jock program. I was a swimmer."

His speech on *Speaker's Corner* caught the attention of Warner Brothers, and in two weeks they gave him a call.

Would you like to try out for the role, Mr. Speedman?

Scott indeed read for the role. Although he didn't get the part (that went to Chris O'Donnell), the casting director was impressed enough by his abilities that he recommended him to an agent.

Scott's career began.

His first film was a short one called *Can I Get a Witness?*

He went on to appear in TV in episodes of *Kung Fu: The Legend Continues*, *Nancy Drew*, and *Goosebumps*.

Scott also did some films, mostly for TV, such as *Net Worth*, *Giant Mine*, *Ursa Major*, *Dead Silence*, *Whatever Happened to Bobby Earl?*, and *Every Nine Seconds*.

However, it was possibly his work in an independent film that brought him to the attention of the producers of *Felicity*.

That film was a Canadian production called *Kitchen Party*.

KITCHEN PARTY

In this low-budget but high-laugh movie, Scott Speedman stars in the lead role as Scott, a suburban teen who wants to have a party at his house with his friends.

''That's the one I'm really proud of. I think it's a really good movie and it's so fun to watch,'' he told the *Calgary Sun*.

In the plot, Scott's character's parents are going to another party that night, a supper party. His reclusive older brother, Steve, just stays in the basement, listening to loud rock music.

Scott's mother has said it's okay to have friends

over, but they have to stay in the kitchen. All the rest of the clean house is off-limits.

The film is a comedy with a dark edge about how things go entirely wrong at both parties, thanks to too much drinking at both.

Gary Burns, the director, got his bachelor of fine arts in film production at Concordia University in Canada and has made many award-winning short films. *The Suburbanators* was his first full-length film and it has been shown at festivals around the world.

"The dialogue sparkles throughout and the situations surrounding the characters are humorous and/or dramatic without ever feeling contrived," said Tyler McLeod in the *Calgary Sun*.

Mike Boon at the *Calgary Herald* announced that "Burns understands the relationships teens have with their parents and each other, transforming what could have been a routine low-budget comedy into an engaging slice-of-life affair."

The film also got a nice write-up in *Variety*.

"For the most part this is a remarkably funny slice of teen angst filmmaking that should elicit interest from specialized U.S. distribs," suggested Brendan Kelly.

It did.

Kitchen Party—perhaps thanks to Scott Speedman's newfound celebrity buzz—made its American debut just about the same time as *Felicity* was warming up TV screens.

It sounds like a film worth going to see.

SCOTT IN PRIVATE

When the casting folk of *Felicity* heard about this handsome talented actor, Scott was living at his mom's in Toronto, sleeping on the couch.

"I auditioned on videotape and I sent it down," says Scott in *Teen People*. "A week later they called me up and said they wanted me, [based on] the tape. It was on a Wednesday and I flew down on Thursday, met Keri on Sunday and we started shooting on Monday."

Curiously enough, the character on the show he is most struck by is Felicity.

"I had a crush on a girl for a couple of years in high school. I eventually started dating her, but for two years I just followed her around and watched her," Scott reveals in the November 1998 issue of *In Style* magazine.

When you read about Scott, or watch him in interviews, you get the impression of a really laid-back guy.

"He's the only person I've ever met without an agenda," said costar Scott Foley of him during a chat on *E! Online*.

Scott doesn't have a girlfriend, although he says

that if he really knew a girl like Felicity, he would definitely date her.

He likes women who are independent.

Lots of actors hang out in their trailers between takes.

Not Scott Speedman.

"I can't sit in those trailers," he told *Teen People*. "I like to watch what's going on or walk around. I walk a lot."

Teen People also has a picture of him playing basketball, which he likes to do between scenes. But his favorite exercise is apparently walking.

"I walk so much, people think I'm nuts," he told *TV Guide*.

Since he hasn't had a girlfriend for a while, he's probably been walking around a lot!

When Scott's not walking (in used jeans, which are his fave pants) he likes TV (his favorite TV series is a Canadian production that airs on PBS called *The News Room*), movies, particularly those by Peter Weir (who just directed *The Truman Show* and is famous for *Dead Poets' Society* and *Picnic at Hanging Rock*).

The movie *Dazed and Confused* is also high on his list of faves, probably partly because of its classic-rock sound track. (Other classic-rock favorites of Scott's include Led Zeppelin and Neil Young.)

Scott also likes to read. While talking to *TV Guide*, he was reading *The Best of Roald Dahl*. Dahl's short stories, not his famous children's books (*Charlie and the Chocolate Factory, James and the Giant Peach.*). Good choice. Dahl was a clever writer and wrote some dark, funny gems.

He's also a fan of Jack Kerouac, the "Beat Generation" novelist of the 1950s. "I'd love to have a couple of drinks with Jack Kerouac. *On the Road* is kind of a bible for my generation," he says of Kerouac's most famous novel in *In Style.*

When *Felicity*'s producer's cast Scott, his resemblance to Matthew McConaughey was noted. However, with the shaded performance this guy's been giving as Ben Covington, he may make people forget that comparison.

Plus, never forget!

E! Online gave Scott a full 10 out of 10 on their "Angel Attainability" chart.

"He's got it," they say.

Whether he gets Felicity remains to be seen!

SEVEN

Amy's Aim

In a recent online chat after the airing of the first episode of *Felicity*, an outraged viewer asked Amy Jo Johnson why she'd stolen Felicity's man!

Amy Jo responded that she didn't write the show. She just acted in it.

It's easy to see how fans can become confused. Amy Jo is really, really good at acting the role of Julie Emrick.

Although the show is certainly not *Julie,* Amy Jo's character is featured prominently. She seems a little more worldly than Felicity, and probably has more experience. But Julie also seems more reserved and careful than Felicity—you get the feeling that she's been hurt, and wants to protect herself.

Amy Jo's acting is perfect for the role, and it's

certain that she will continue being featured prominently in the series.

Amy Jo's been working on acting for a while and it shows.

THIS IS YOUR LIFE, AMY JO

If there was a rumor on the Internet that Amy Jo Johnson somersaulted into life, don't believe it.

The actress, famous for her ability in gymnastics, actually used a mini-trampoline.

Seriously, folks . . .

On October 5, 1970, Amy Jo Johnson was born just like any other baby, in Cape Cod, Massachusetts.

Whether or not she was a bouncing baby or a jumping tyke, no one can say, except perhaps her parents, her sister, Julie Clary, or brother, Grieg (named after her father Grieg).

However, it is on record that at age seven she began her gymnastics career at the Cape Cod Gymnastics School. Whether or not she fantasized herself in a superhero role, she was good at rolling and tumbling, climbing and jumping to such an extent that she participated not only in local but national and international gymnastic shows until her sophomore year at Dennis-Yarmouth Regional High.

Amy Jo had always been fascinated with acting.

She started when she was eleven years old, and played the title role of Annie in a school production of the musical. She continued to work in school drama, but was always overshadowed by other aspiring young actors and tended to get dinky roles, she told the Amy Jo Johnson Fan Club, because "my really good friend since I was about four, Katy Coogan, was always better than me. She has an awesome voice."

While still in high school, Amy Jo was a finalist in the Miss Teen Massachusetts pageant. She was sixteen years old at the time. Also in those high-school years she worked with the Orleans Academy Playhouse.

After high school, like Felicity, she moved to New York. There she studied at the Lee Strasberg Theater Institute.

Like many other aspiring actresses, Amy Jo thought that L.A. might be a possible option, so after New York she made the brave move of heading for the West Coast.

Los Angeles, however, was at first a no-go. She hated it. She moved back to New York, where she continued her Felicity-style experience.

However, Amy Jo Johnson had long since learned the gymnastics skill of bouncing back.

So she gave Los Angeles one more try.

Within weeks, she snagged the role that would hurtle her into fame . . .

DINO-AMY

Amy's first on-screen role was as Kimberly Ann Hart, one of Saban Entertainment's *Mighty Morphin Power Rangers*.

"I went to eight or nine auditions," she told *TV Guide*'s online Web site, *TVGEN*, held in a Yahoo! chatroom. "I think my gymnastics background really helped me get the job."

Kimberly is the "Pink Ranger," a teenager who's been gifted by the alien Zordon with Pterodactyl Power and who flies a Pterodactyl Dino-Zord—basically a cool robot with wings, in pure Japanese "mecha" tradition. She, along with her five other fellow Power Rangers, fights to keep the world safe from monsters.

Of course, *Power Rangers* was a Japanese television series cleverly adapted to include American TV actors and story lines. Much of its success was due not only to Amy's charm—but also to the fact that it was nothing less than a live-action cartoon, and kids loved it.

Amy appeared on the show for three seasons, from 1993 to 1995.

The *Power Rangers* also featured Amy's first on-screen kiss—with fellow ranger Jason David Frank. (As all *Felicity* fans know, Amy's had more on-screen kisses since—and she seems to know what she's doing.)

Although it was "hot and stuffy" inside the

Power Ranger outfit, Amy didn't always have the pink thing on, often battling bad guys and delivering her dialogue as a civilian.

During the course of the *Power Rangers,* Kimberly developed from an airheaded materialist to a caring, compassionate person. When Amy Jo decided to leave the show, her character, Kimberly, left as well to train for the PanGlobal Games.

However, before this decision she had time to star in two movies besides three seasons' worth of shows!

PINK MOVIE STAR

If you're not familiar with the *Power Rangers* and would like to see Amy Jo in glorious athletic action, you couldn't get a better start than this:

Mighty Morphin Power Rangers: The Movie

Okay. Even if you don't really want to check out the *Power Rangers,* this is worth taking a look at in your video store, if only to see what the fuss was all about.

This film is pretty much pure rollicking action from titles to credits and beyond. But it's also a barrel of fun and laughs and not necessarily just for kids. (Although kids, of course, were the target audience.)

And Amy Jo not only shows off her gymnastic and martial-arts prowess—she's gets to act.

This one concerns the evil Lord Ooze, who Kimberly's boss and the teen rangers of yesteryear imprisoned millennia earlier in a special egg-shaped chamber. After being unearthed by construction workers and reinvigorated by Zedd and company, Lord Ooze (vigorously acted by Paul Freeman) imprisons the good guys and tears about the Rangers' headquarters. To save the Rangers' leader and Earth, the Rangers must travel to a distant, fantastic, and dangerous planet and bring back a marvelous power.

As Kimberly, the Pink Ranger, Amy Jo is pretty darned wonderful in this one. Whether in her Pterodactyl Ranger suit guise, or in her blouse and shorts and bobby tail, our Amy is chipper and alert, whether skydiving or jumping or nailing a bad guy with a karate kick.

Such is her star power that even one of the villains thinks she's cute.

If you're a *Felicity* fan and want to see one of its stars in a former life, watch *Mighty Morphin Power Rangers: The Movie*.

Besides, that way you'll understand the joke in *Felicity*'s Halloween episode!

SWITCH TO TURBO

If you liked the first movie, you'll enjoy the second as well.

Here, the Rangers get special turbo powers and ''TurboZord'' vehicles in order to fight yet another threat to Earth, this time in the form of the space pirate Divatox.

Nasty Divatox, it seems, wants to free the grim critter Maligore from its island prison of Mirantias. A nice wizard named Lariget has the key—and the Rangers must help him keep it away from Divatox.

TEEN ANGEL

In *Susie Q,* which appeared on TV on October 3, 1996, Amy Jo played the character of Susie Quinn, who is killed in a car crash in the 1950s.

No silly songs were written about Susie, but when her parents go broke forty years later, she comes back as a teen angel to help them out. Back on Earth, she also has the chance to help out a confused, fatherless teen.

HIGH-SCHOOL HIJINKS

Before she got the part of Julie on *Felicity,* Amy Jo's favorite role was in a TV movie called *Killing Mr. Griffin* for NBC.

"It was the first part I had gotten that didn't have anything to do with my gymnastics ability," she explained during her *TVgen* interview. "It was exciting to get a part just from my acting talent."

Killing Mr. Griffin, based on the 1960s young-adult novel of the same name, casts Amy Jo as Susan McConnell, a shy, plain high-school girl who has a crush on a fellow student, Dave Ruggles, who is played by Mario Lopez. Susan gets involved in the shenanigans of a group of popular students who decide that it would be a wonderful prank to kidnap Mr. Griffin of the high school and videotape the whole proceedings. Unfortunately, plans go wrong—horribly wrong—and the group, including Susan, must face the consequences.

Killing Mr. Griffin aired on April 7, 1997.

Although Amy Jo had the lead role in this TV flick, she didn't get top billing.

One of the interesting things about the role, though, was that her character was very much like that of Felicity!

Could it be possible that this was the role that caught the attention of the producers of that Touchstone show?

Maybe Amy Jo auditioned for the role of Felicity before she auditioned for the role of Julie!

ANOTHER BODY

In *Perfect Body*, a TV movie for NBC, this one airing September 8, 1997, Amy Jo played a fifteen-year-old.

Even though the role called for her to be much younger than she actually was (like the *Felicity* role of Julie), it was nonetheless very true to life. The character she plays, Andie Braden, is a gymnast, just like Amy Jo was at the time.

("I don't practice [gymnastics] now," she said recently on the *TVgen* online chat. "But I love to watch it on TV.")

High-schooler Andie Braden has got a lot to be thankful for at the beginning of the movie. She does well in school, has a nice boyfriend, and a promising gymnastics career, with a shot at the Olympics. However, when she gets a top-flight women's gymnastics coach to help her, Andie quickly learns that the coach's star pupil is bulimic . . . bingeing then purging herself to stay trim for competition. Andie eats very little in order to stay at the weight the coach wants her at—but then becomes ill. Instead of going ahead and harming herself, Andie decides to give up the Olympics road—and go back to being a happy, healthy teenager.

For this movie, Amy Jo was listed at the top of the credits bill.

And you can certainly see how it led to her next role . . . This time for something on the big screen.

WITHOUT LIMITS LIMITED

Without Limits is one of several movies that have recently been made about Steve Prefontaine, the University of Oregon student runner who wowed the world in the early seventies—and then died young in a car crash.

In this version of the story, generally seen by critics as the superior dramatization, Billy Crudup plays Prefontaine as a stubborn, proud perfectionist determined to win—and make each race a work of art. Directed and written by Robert Townsend, the film features Donald Sutherland, excellent in the role of "Pre's" coach.

It also stars Amy Jo Johnson in a small, but memorable part as a gymnast from Idaho who catches Steve Prefontaine's eye while bouncing on a trampoline.

The two enjoy an unusual and short romance, which features Amy Jo performing a most unusual gymnastic stunt that, alas, results in a foot injury to the runner. Prefontaine, however, despite stitches, soldiers on and wins his next race.

Without Limits is a moving, believable film—and it's good to see Amy Jo show her stuff, despite the size of her role.

CHILLING BLOOD PUMPS

Coming soon to your neighborhood theaters (or perhaps your neighborhood video channels) is a film called *Cold Hearts*, staring Amy Jo, which is supposed to do for vampires what *Scream* did for teenagers.

The film takes place in a mysterious area of the New Jersey shore.

Amy Jo plays Alicia, best friend to Viktoria, a girl who has got a big problem.

A former vampire-lore fan, Viktoria is now a

vampire herself. The poor girl suffers from all sorts of identity problems and is trying to be good, but when other vampires enter the picture, both she and Alicia get into very bad trouble.

The famous Tom Savini is supposed to be supplying vampire special effects.

And to make things all the more "authentic," Nicholas Brendan, of *Buffy the Vampire Slayer,* is also cast in the movie.

Cold Hearts is an independent production from How Bad Productions.

Hopefully, after *Felicity* fans see it, they'll be talking about HOW GOOD Amy Jo is in the flick.

Future Films?

One of Amy's goals for the next few years is to do more feature films. She'd love to work for Disney, but would rather stay away from the horror films that are so popular these days. And if the Power Rangers come knocking again?

Well, she's decided that she's past all that now.

Still, thanks to the excellence of her performance in *Felicity,* our bet is that Amy Jo Johnson will be in more movies soon.

eight

Kicking Back with Amy Jo

Okay.

You're on the famous Sunset Strip in Los Angeles. You've just hit Book Soup, where you grabbed hold of this volume (smart buy!) and you're headed into Tower Records across the street.

Lots of cool cars drive by, and it smells like exhaust mixed with eucalyptus leaves. Inside the famous record stores are piles of the new *L.A. Weekly,* the free L.A. newspaper. You're wondering what to do tonight after your dinner at Spago just a hop away—nah, let's make it Hamburger Hamlet!—and the *Weekly* has a great listing of what's on at the hot spots.

You look through the listing of famous music venues, like the Roxy and the Whiskey and the Roxbury . . .

And there it is.

Awesome!
Valhalla is playing tonight!

One of the great things about L.A. is that you sometimes get to see stars out and about. Usually, it's not in limos either. They're jogging up near Mulholland Drive or watering their lawn or maybe just getting milk and bread at the neighborhood Ralph's Supermarket.

Most of the time they're on a TV set or a movie set, doing their jobs, of course, but there are always extracurricular activities.

Take Amy Jo, for instance. She's got a rock band that plays around the area, and if you were in L.A. you could go see her play.

The name of the band is Valhalla. Amy is the lead guitarist and lead singer.

When asked by a fan on the *TVgen* chat what her greatest achievement was, she responded, "Teaching myself to play guitar enough to be able to play around Hollywood with real great musicians."

And Amy Jo has reason to be proud. Apparently she did all this in just three years. Her character Julie also plays guitar, so maybe we'll see Julie forming a band on *Felicity*. That would be a great story line!

Last year, between acting jobs, A. J. (whoops! . . . that's the name that only good friends call her!) spent a lot of time working with Valhalla, gigging around the L.A. area at such cool spots as Bar Deluxe. Although Valhalla rocks out, to be sure, they like to experiment with what Amy Jo calls "acid-folk."

Maybe Valhalla will get famous enough to start playing around the country in big halls and we can all get to see them.

In any case, you definitely get the feeling that the cast members of *Felicity* really like Amy Jo. Her best friends on the show so far are Keri Russell and Scott Speedman, but there are no reports whatsoever of any kind of friction with other folks on the show.

In fact, one of the fun things cast members like to do is to go out and catch a gig by Valhalla and then hang out afterward.

You get the impression that Amy Jo is a good person to hang out with. She has that sparkle in her eye, that sense of fun . . . And she clearly likes other people.

What are her hobbies?

Obviously guitar playing isn't a hobby anymore—it's a profession. But Amy Jo does still have a few things that keep her occupied in her private time. She loves to collect books. And she also has a big collection of plays. When she first started surfing the net, after looking at the Web sites dedicated to her (she found the fake nudes of her really silly), she headed to a site to find out what she could about what dramas were playing in New York City so she could decide what to see.

She loves to read. Her favorite books are *Summer Sisters* by Judy Blume and *A Prayer for Owen Meany* by John Irving.

She's a big movie fan.

Her fave movie is *Harold and Maude*

Second favorite: *Cinema Paradiso*.

She loves music, and her favorite singer is Natalie Merchant. Other musicians she digs include The Dave Matthews Band, The Grateful Dead, Peter Gabriel, Andreas Vollenwieder, and "a whole bunch of 'stuff.' "

That includes a band called Date with Dizzy, which is a friend's band—and her favorite.

One of Amy Jo's deepest and most private loves is painting.

Is this woman talented, or what?

CLOSE TO AMY JO

When asked by a fan once (on the *Entertainment Asylum* Web site) what three words would best describer her, she replied, "Silly. Caring. Animal-lover."

The animal she loves the most?

Probably her dog Lucy, a pit bull.

But what's it like to be really close to Amy. Like, does she have a boyfriend?

And does she date anyone on the set of *Felicity*?

She certainly has kissed actors (remember Jason David Frank, her first kiss in *Power Rangers*?).

According to Amy Jo in a recent magazine article, though, one of her most embarrassing kisses ever occurred with an actor during a scene in *Perfect Body*. After the smooch, she was so nervous that she impulsively told the actor he smelled like kitty pee—when he didn't!

It's nice to see that smart, sassy, and with-it Amy Jo can be nervous, too. Certainly she's gotten a lot of ribbing in Hollywood about being a Power Ranger. She's in with the in-crowd now, but it wasn't always so. In high school, she felt like an "outcast." Her achievements as a gymnast were all that made her feel "normal."

In the January 1999 issue of *YM*, she talks about her very first kiss:

"I was sixteen. My first boyfriend and I were in his basement watching a movie. The kiss was wonderful. I felt like electricity was running through my whole body."

Amy Jo's first boyfriend was probably on her mind because he'd just called her before the interview. Now's he's married with kids. Not with Amy Jo, of course!

According to an interview as recent as last year, with members of the Amy Jo Johnson Fan Club, Amy Jo was engaged to a man named Colin.

At the time her favorite thing to do was to curl up with Colin, eat ice cream, and watch *Nick at Nite*.

However, when someone asked her recently

about her personal life, she said that was her private business.

In *YM*, though, she reported herself still single and searching. "I'll wait for my knight. I'm not giving up!"

Presumably this means that she's not engaged anymore, right?

So again, the question is—is she dating one of those guys on the cast or the set . . . like maybe one of the two hunky Scotts?

She told a fan during a recent online chat that she was not.

Another fan asked her to marry her.

Amy Jo declined.

You get the feeling that Amy Jo wants to work on her career very hard—but that she's also a deeply romantic and open person.

In fact, she says that what she shows on TV while acting really isn't her.

"Julie is very reserved," she said to Julie Trelling of *YM*. "But I wear my heart on my sleeve, more like Felicity."

You can't help wishing this woman a really good life and lots of roles . . .

And I, for one, would love to see her play with her band!

Greet Scott!

FROM *DAWSON* TO AWESOME

Who can forget the premise?

Shy girl gives up earlier college plans and chooses to go to college on another coast to follow a guy she thinks likes her because he signed her high-school yearbook in a way that seemed to show feelings for her.

That gorgeous guy who signed that yearbook and started a TV series was Ben Covington. And Ben was always Scott Speedman, right?

Wrong!

Scott Foley was going to play Ben.

That's right! Noel was going to be Ben?

Confused? Well, here's what went down.

Once Keri Russell was cast in the lead, the show

was a go. Amy Jo Johnson was perfect for Julie, and so that was no problem.

However, the guys . . . well, they weren't quite so easy to find.

Have you ever wondered who chooses the people to play roles in TV and movies? Yeah, the producers, of course . . . But who finds the people to show to the producer? It's a talent and skill to spot the right people or roles and that's why there are special people to do this: casting directors.

The casting director for The WB, Marsha Schulman, was the person who found James Van Der Beek, Katie Holmes, Josh Jackson, and Michelle Williams for *Dawson's Creek*. And she'd also turned up an actor named Scott Foley to play Cliff, an admirer of Jen for a few episodes in the first season.

When they auditioned Scott Foley, Marsha Schulman and the producers thought they had found Mr. Right to play Ben. But then, as they started looking for the fly guy to play Noel Crane, Felicity's resident adviser, they came up empty-handed.

But when they found someone else who could play Ben—someone with the looks, the sensitivity, and the pizzazz—they called Scott Foley in for a meeting.

"They sit me down and I'm thinking 'Oh, man, I'm getting fired!' " Scott Foley told *Entertainment Weekly*. The news about Scott Speedman landing the role of Ben was soon announced. But they couldn't find someone to play Noel. " 'We know you can do both. So would you play him?' At that point, I'm just happy that I still have a job. I'm like, 'Yes . . . of course! Anything! Can I empty your garbage?' "

THE FIRST NOEL

Noel is clearly a little older and more responsible than the other characters. He happens to be a resident adviser at Felicity's dorm.

Noel has a crush on Felicity.

"There's something in his eyes when he first sees her and something clicks. He knows that she could be the one," Scott told a WB interviewer for their *Dawson's Creek* WebPage.

Scott himself had a similar experience. Riding away from a Fourth of July fireworks display in the back of a Jeep, he got stuck in a traffic jam. He shook the hand of a girl sitting on a motorcycle by the Jeep. Their eyes met and something clicked. Scott believes that sometimes people have this kind of instantaneous connection. Although the event with the girl on the motorcycle happened seven years ago, he still remembers it well.

Scott Foley plays Noel just right.

He's a guy who thinks . . . and feels . . . a lot.

Would Scott Foley rather have stayed on as Ben?

"No," he told *E! Online*. "I was thrilled to be

cast as Ben. I'm much happier in the role of Noel. He's a more developed person, move evolved. He's a year older and he's been in college a year longer than [the others]. I seem to have more in common with Noel. And Noel gets to kiss Felicity!''

That's the feeling you get about Scott Foley.

And you also get the feeling that he's got a terrific sense of humor.

Who is this guy, though, and how did he end up on *Felicity*?

BIO

Scott Foley was born twenty-six years ago in Kansas City, Missouri.

He didn't stay there long, though.

His father worked in international banking, so Scott lived in places all over the world.

"I moved around a lot when I was younger," he told Wanda on *E! Online*. "Australia, Hawaii, the Mainland. I couldn't play football in Australia. I had to play rugby."

While traveling, Scott's companions were TV sets and movies, so he always wanted to be like the people he saw there—actors!

During the fourth grade, he appeared in his first play. He had to sing "I'd Do Anything" from the musical *Oliver!* in front of the whole school.

From that day forward, that's all he wanted to do.

"I have younger brothers and we relied on each other for whatever we needed, whether it was entertainment or support," he said in an interview for The WB *Dawson's Creek* WebPage. His father was very supportive of Scott's desire to act. "He said, 'If you love what you're doing it's not work, so find something you love doing and do it well.' That's my dad."

Scott did get back Stateside long enough to attend high school in St. Louis, Missouri . . . Long enough, presumably, not only to play football, but to get a taste of teenage life in America.

Acting in regional theater since he was twelve, Scott definitely had the acting bug.

In fact, he had it so bad, after high school, when he heard that Los Angeles was the place to go, he hopped a plane with only a one-way ticket, even though he knew absolutely nothing about the place.

He got to know L.A. a lot better.

For six years, while honing his craft and trying to get auditions, he earned his living waiting tables in L.A. restaurants.

Then, in 1997, he got his big break, landing an agent.

Within a month he got work.

On *E! Online*, he reports, "My first acting job—paying acting job—was a movie with Yasmine Bleeth and I was a valet called Matt. It was called *Broken Crown*."

Not long afterward Scott got his break.

He auditioned for—and got—a role on the teen breakthrough series of the late nineties . . . *Dawson's Creek*.

THE *DAWSON* EPISODES

On *Dawson's Creek*, Scott played the role of Cliff, the all-American football player who vied with Dawson for Jen's affection.

Scott had signed for three episodes. But he was so good that he did an additional two.

Dawson's Creek, in case you've been living in Tokyo—no, make that Siberia—no, make that Neptune . . . *DC,* as it is affectionately called, is a hugely popular new show.

It tells of the trials and tribulations of a group of teens who live in Capeside, a small town near the ocean not too far from Boston. These are Dawson (James Van Der Beek), Joey (Katie Holmes), Pacey (Josh Jackson), and Jen (Michelle Williams).

It's a clever show that looks into character interaction with a depth that few series with continuing story lines (can you say "soaps"?) reach—yet with snappy dialogue and hip allusions to pop culture that make the characters seem absolutely vivid and real.

If you haven't done so yet, start watching. There's lots of time to think about plot and action and catch up on things while the characters kiss (they do this often).

"We all got along amazingly well," says Scott of his fellow actors on *Dawson's Creek* in his interview with The WB'S *Dawson's Creek* WebPage. Since Scott was older than the others, in a way he was like a big brother to them, and they would often come to him seeking help and advice about their roles.

What about the character of Cliff?

"Cliff was the high school quarterback, all-American jock, honor society, goes to church, the girls-love-him guy," Scott told The WB *Dawson's Creek* WebPage.

Cliff was much more self-confident than Dawson, but as Dawson matured, Cliff actually asked for Dawson's opinions.

Scott reports that though Josh Jackson (Pacey) was the big prankster on the set, he didn't bother Scott . . . Scott was bigger than him!

However, now that Josh has grown, Cliff suspects that he'd get a great deal of good-natured trouble if they ever worked together again.

Dawson's Creek is happily into its second season, but without Cliff, who morphed into *Felicity*'s Noel.

He was written out of the plot and, according to Scott, will not return.

Who does he actually prefer personally of the two *DC* gals—Jen or Joey?

"I love both Katie and Michelle. But character-

wise . . . Joey,'' Scott is on the record as saying on
E! Online.

One of the way cool things about what's been
going on in his life lately is that now Scott numbers
the *Dawson* gang as some of his best pals.

THAT FOLEY SMILE

So.

Now that *Felicity* is a hit and he's a regularly
working actor, are things different for Scott?

''The funny thing is that in LA no one cares,''
Scott told *E! Online*. ''So I'm coping just fine.
Nothing's changed.''

Well, not exactly nothing.

For one thing, he doesn't have to wait tables
anymore.

For another, he's got a little more money.

Recently he bought himself a TV. A big TV.
And he's been taking weekend trips around California for fun and relaxation. That's what success
has gotten him so far.

But what about his personal life?

So, Scott? Are those kisses with Keri real?

''No,'' he told *E! Online*. ''Keri and I are great
friends. She's had a boyfriend for quite a while.''

So what about you?

''I'm single, but I'm always looking, always de-
veloping crushes,'' he told a Chat attendee on the
Web recently (*E! Online*).

This doesn't look like it came out of Felicity's wardrobe! Keri Russell at a *Malibu Shores* party.

Is it Ben and Felicity on a date? No, it's Scott Speedman and Keri Russell promoting the show together.

Wonder who he's buying this for? Scott Foley at Frederick's of Hollywood.

Amy Jo Johnson strutting her stuff at the premiere of *Without Limits*. She has the leg thing down pat!

Tangi Miller, beautiful and glamorous at the premiere of *Beloved*.

Photo © 1998 by Lisa Rose/Globe Photos, Inc.

Devon Gummersall looking dapper at the fifth AMC Gala Festival in L.A.

Photo © 1997 by Fitzroy Barrett/Globe Photos, Inc.

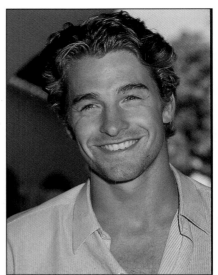

Scott Speedman showing why his character is dubbed "The Stud."

Scott Foley getting up close and personal with Keri Russell and Scott Speedman.

This is apparently a recent occurrence. According to another quote in *TV Guide*, being fully single just happened. Scott just broke up with a girlfriend.

You'd think that a good-looking, personable guy with a sense of humor would have an easy time with girls.

Apparently, though, Scott doesn't. Again, he finds a lot in common with Noel. He said in an interview that they both get nervous around women.

However, he certainly has friends. Although there have been no reported romances on the set of *Felicity,* there have been lots of rumors about good friendships!

Scott says that there's a lot of kidding on the set, but in hard times the actors support each other.

Although he had to wait awhile for success and pay his dues, it looks as though even if *Felicity* had not taken off like it did, Scott would have become a star. He was in the pilot of the upcoming mid-season replacement sitcom *Zoe Bean,* which has been called a young *Seinfeld* and looks to be a hit.

Now that he's locked into place on *Felicity,* he's going to be in only one additional episode as that character.

What does Scott Foley like to do when he's not on the set or talking to his fans or TV reporters?

For one thing, he loves the ocean. He thoroughly enjoys sailing.

He probably plays basketball a lot with Scott

Speedman between scenes, since he loves basketball. Sportswise, he also goes in for tennis and running.

His favorite musicians are Kenny Loggins and Alana Davis, both of whom he listens to wearing his Levi's.

On TV he seldom misses *ER* or Bob Vila's *Home Again*.

His favorite movies are *Forrest Gump* and *St. Elmo's Fire*.

When *TV Guide* caught up with him, he was reading Ralph Ellison's classic *Invisible Man*, which he describes as being "about prejudice and the way someone feels who's being discriminated against." He's also a fan of Daniel Defoe's *Robinson Crusoe*.

Recently, when asked the one word to describe himself and the rest of the *Felicity* cast, he was able to come up with an answer very quickly.

The word was:

Busy!

ten

That Tangi Tang

CITY GIRL

Elena Tyler is one tough cookie.

On the outside, anyway.

Elena's the only one of the five featured characters who was born and raised in New York City. She knows the ropes, she's got a tough skin—and she's forward and direct.

When she thinks that Felicity has gotten one of the coveted mini-refrigerators because of a special romantic ''in'' with the dorm resident adviser Noel, Elena makes no bones about it. She marches straight in and confronts Felicity.

She's seen lots more of New York, of course, than the other characters and has that ''New York crust.'' When Felicity and Ben are robbed, Elena tells about her mugging two years before—at knife-point. But she talks about it as a rite of passage, not as something particularly unusual.

"Some people might consider her a b-i-t-c-h," Tangi Miller tells *Teen People*. "But I think she's just direct."

There's another side to Elena, though.

She's smart, for one thing. And opinionated! An admitted jazz freak, she thinks the linchpin of modern jazz—Charlie Parker—is overrated.

And she also has her vulnerable side. When Elena impulsively becomes involved with a cute guy in a Tin Man outfit she meets at a Halloween party—Blair—she probably thinks it's just a wild fling. But then she has a hard time brushing him off.

When she stops an elevator mid-ride to demand that Felicity give her advice, Felicity suggests that she might really like Blair. (And Felicity also promises future advice, without a kidnapping being necessary.)

Elena is the kind of girl who'd you be scared of at first—but then realize is a wonderful person—and a valuable friend.

What does it take to play this kind of character?

IMPORTANT FACT

Can you guess what one of the big differences between Tangi Miller and the other cast members of *Felicity* is?

Well, yes, true, she's African American, but that's not what I'm talking about.

BEEP! Sorry. Time's up!

Tangi's the only member of the cast who's actually finished college! (Scott Speedman attended the University of Toronto awhile, but didn't like it.) In fact, she's got a bachelor's degree and a master's degree.

Of course, you don't have to have been a college student to play a college student. You just have to look young. However, it's nice to know that one of the actors on the show has had real experience with academic term papers and mid-semester exams and dorms and fraternities and sororities and all the elements of college that can be expected on a campus light-years from a Hollywood studio.

Tangi Miller was born twenty-eight years ago in Miami, Florida, where she grew up.

Her acting experience at a younger age included many high-school productions.

She twirled baton for sports events, and was a class president in high school.

However, although she excelled and loved the craft of acting, when she did go to college, she thought she should apply herself to something more practical.

For that reason, Tangi decided to major in marketing. She went to Alabama State University, where she got that bachelor's degree we mentioned.

However, the acting bug was still there, so she

decided to run with it. First she hopped over to the University of California, Irvine, where she got herself that masters of fine arts.

You'd think that after that, a person would immediately get herself a Hollywood agent and start going to casting calls. But no . . . not Tangi. She felt she had more to learn.

So she went to London, where she studied at the Royal National Theatre. She must have done a lot of Shakespeare plays (all those British actors do, don't they?) because when she got back she immediately appeared at the Alabama Shakespeare Festival.

Then Tangi decided have a go at something besides theater.

Tangi almost immediately landed a few roles in independent features, including *Tears of a Clown* and *Rhinos.*

Her TV work in HBO's *Arliss* and CBS's *Michael Hayes* was what lined her up for a shot at a continuing character.

And that is just what Tangi got.

Here's how!

CASTING GROUCH

When WB executives first saw the pilot for *Felicity,* the character of Elena Tyler was, of course, no place to be seen.

However, the character of Julie, as played by

Amy Jo Johnson, was very much in evidence, and The WB executives were concerned.

Julie wasn't a particularly important character in the first episode (certainly not as important as she later became as Felicity's friend and confidante). The creators had been so interested in creating a fascinating female lead character that they'd skimped on the development of the secondary characters. WB executives weren't impressed by Amy Jo.

However, J. J. and Matt truly believed in Amy Jo, and they stood their ground when executives at the network wanted to find another actress for the part. They won and Amy Jo stayed—and now The WB executives are thrilled with the job that Amy Jo Johnson is doing and the way the writers have developed the character of Julie.

The executives, though, did have a suggestion.

With all these out-of-towners in the cast, why not put in a New Yorker—a streetwise sort, who could play off the sweet but "white bread" qualities of the other characters?

This surely would add conflict.

The producers agreed, and a fifth person was added to the main cast—and since all the other characters were so clearly majority Americans, why not make the character an important minority?

Thus, Tangi Miller, talented Afro-American, became a regular, whose images are seen in nice dissolving photos during the opening part of the show.

TANGI, A LITTLE BLURRY

Because she was such a late addition, Tangi Miller's not as well known to *Felicity* fans as the other actors.

No doubt, hopefully, that will change.

However, there are a few glimpses available of Tangi Miller as a private person.

For one thing, she gets along great with the other actors in the cast, and hangs out with them.

She's brought another popular addition to the *Felicity* set: a beautiful parrot named Tekay, to whom she's always teaching new tricks. (Check out a picture of Tangi and Tekay in the November issue of *Teen People*.)

For another, she has a rule about dating members of any production she's working on.

"You hear about people falling in love on sets. My rule is, if you like someone, wait until six months after a [kissing] scene to [date]," she tells *YM* magazine.

So! Here's one person who might actually think about dating another actor on *Felicity*?

Not necessarily.

Tangi, it seems, has a boyfriend.

"My boyfriend," she reports in *YM,* "says I'm starting to act like Elena. But I'm not as together as she is. I wish I were, though."

Tangi seems like an actress to watch.

I certainly look forward to the further adventures of Elena Tyler—but I'd also like to learn more about Tangi Miller.

eLeveN

The Pink Guy

One of the funniest (and most lifelike) scenes on *Felicity* concerned Felicity and Julie doing their laundry. Yes, their laundry! You don't see that too much on *Beverly Hills 90210*!

Anyway, as they were sorting out their wash, and their relationship, they met a guy named Zach, who needed help. All his clothes had just turned pink. He holds up his underwear—and it's pink! He thinks that someone has put food coloring into his wash. Julie informs him that you really shouldn't put a new red sweatshirt into a pile of "light" clothing. Apparently, Zach's mom always did his laundry at home.

Zach's a shy, introverted film student who's making his own short feature. He invites Julie to see what he has shot so far—and it's the start of a friendship that turned sour.

When Zach appeared on-screen, many *Felicity* fans recognized the actor.

"It's Brian Krakow," they said. "From *My So-Called Life!*"

In fact, the truth is that it's the actor who played Brian Krakow on *My So-Called Life,* Devon Gummersall. He's grown since then, and that definitely curly hair is shorter, but yep, that's Devon.

YOUNG TV AND MOVIE STAR

Of all the talented actors on *Felicity,* Devon was the one who started acting in TV and films first. He was aged ten and mostly appeared in commercials about food.

Devon was born on October 15, 1978, in Durango, Colorado. His father is the artist C. Gregory Gummersall, and Devon is the second of three boys.

One of the first guest appearances Devon made was on the NBC sitcom *Blossom.* He's appeared in many other series, including *Dr. Quinn, Medicine Woman; Step By Step; Peaceable Kingdom;* and *Dream On.*

Movies? You bet. He's appeared in a couple of sequels. *Beethoven's 2nd* and *My Girl 2,* as a matter of fact.

Most folks remember Devon on *My So-Called Life* not only because the show's been repeated on MTV, but because he was so good in the role of

Brian Krakow, an introverted soul. In reality, Devon is not introverted at all, and engages regularly in athletics.

After *My So-Called Life*, Devon appeared in the short-lived series *Relativity* as Jake Roth. His other movie and TV-movie credits include *It's My Party, From the Mixed-Up Files of Mrs. Basil E. Frankweiler, Educating Mom, Independence Day, Do Me a Favor, Lured Innocence,* and *When Trumpets Fade.*

Quite a list!

Devon's family lives in the San Fernando Valley near Los Angeles with a German shepherd named Nick and Feisty, a cat. Devon, since he's twenty now and working, probably doesn't live with them anymore, but he most likely stays in touch.

Devon's into baseball and basketball and has been known to Rollerblade up a storm.

He's a book freak and loved to study literature in high school, where his favorite author was J. D. Salinger. Last time anyone asked about it, his favorite actor was Al Pacino.

Is Devon really going to be a film director like his character Zach in *Felicity*?

We'll see!

twelve

The Show and Its Creators

AFTER THE ALLY CREEK?

It's a fact:

Ally McBeal was a breakout hit about a young woman in transition. Its star, Calista Flockhart, set the media ablaze with her cute face and her sharp acting.

It's a fact:

Dawson's Creek was a breakout hit, featuring exciting new teen actors in compelling drama with a touch of comedy and much hip dialogue against an interesting backdrop.

It's a fact:

Felicity is drama with a sweet dab of comedy about a young girl in transition, featuring teen characters with great dialogue against a background teeming with possibilities.

So. From these facts, can you automatically assume that the Dr. Frankensteins of TV, between sips of Perrier water and Starbucks coffee, manufactured *Felicity* in some studio lab somewhere with the help of bubbly chemicals, electricity, and dug-up writers' brains?

When *Felicity* debuted, lots of reviewers could not help but notice the similarities between it and the other recent hits.

However, if you thought that the creators of the show, J. J. Abrams and Matt Reeves, cynically cobbled together these elements, hurriedly patched up the seams, and then Daffy Duck and Bugs Bunny at Warner Brothers bought them and gave them to projector operator Elmer Fudd to show, you'd be very, very wrong.

It's a fact:

Felicity was created before *Ally McBeal* and *Dawson's Creek* ever aired!

THE BIRTH OF A DREAM

Felicity was born in the South Seas of the Pacific Ocean.

Bali, to be precise.

J. J. Abrams (the first *J* is for John) was on his honeymoon. Whether he was snorkeling in a lagoon or enjoying the sun at the time, only J. J. knows, but during the trip he remembered a high-school girl named Felicity. J. J. had been thinking about doing a coming-of-age screenplay for a while. Since he wrote movies (including *Regarding Henry* and *Armageddon*), he naturally envisioned it as about two hours long and showing in movie-plexes everywhere.

J. J. had a really good friend he'd known since they were kids. This was Matt Reeves, who had just done the movie *The Pallbearer* (with David Schwimmer of *Friends*). J. J. thought that not only would Matt be a great director for the project, he probably would also be able to contribute just the right idea elements to make the movie a hit.

"I always loved the idea of a young woman taking control of her life for the first time," J. J. told a fan on *E! Online*. "And doing it in a spastic way. Realizing she made a big mistake, following a boy. But ultimately taking charge of her life was the right decision."

However, as the two guys stirred their story cauldron, it became magically bigger and bigger.

They both loved the idea, but they realized that this story was simply too big and wonderful for a mere movie.

"Every [movie] version seemed stupid," Abrams told *Time* magazine. "We realized the thing that felt inspiring was this character, the voice of this person who was taking a huge risk and experiencing what it is to make a mistake for the first time and take the consequences."

No, to bring out all the reality and truth they

wanted to show about life, it would have to be a TV series.

So. The elements of the pilot were decided upon, and Abrams jumped into his word-processing cockpit and zoomed.

The result: the pilot script called *Felicity*!

Rumor has it that David E. Kelley (married to Michelle Pfeiffer and super-Hollywood wonderguy creator of *Picket Fences, Chicago Hope,* and *The Practice*) saw it first. However, he was already working on another woman's story.

Ally McBeal's, in fact.

However, just as soon as Imagine Television, a production company headed by such folk as Ron Howard of Opie and *Happy Days* and directorial fame, got a look at the script, they snapped it up.

PRE-*DAWSON* PROOF!

Check it out!

Spring 1997!

That's when Daffy and Bugs first got to look at the pilot script for *Felicity*.

And in spring of 1997 The WB decided that it wanted to buy it.

They had a meeting with *Felicity*'s creators and told them how much they liked it.

However, remember this was before *Dawson's Creek*. The creators, while excited, were concerned about The WB being so small. ABC was interested, but it had just had a flop with *Relativity*.

Thus The WB hooked up with J. J. Abrams and Matt Reeves to start the big TV wheels turning, bound for history.

But first, they needed the most important part of the whole package.

They needed a star for the show!

ENTER KERI

Here's a stunner:

According to *Entertainment Weekly*, in their September 4, 1998, issue, Abrams and Reeves made a courageous decision before they even shot *Felicity*'s pilot.

If they couldn't find the right actress to fill the role, they wouldn't go ahead with the project.

You would think that with all the actresses in Hollywood and New York, where the producers looked, finding the right person would be easy. It wasn't. After auditioning dozens and dozens, they still hadn't found the right girl to play *Felicity*.

Meanwhile, there was another problem. Abrams had chosen New York as the scene of the show, doubtless because it not only offered plenty of opportunity for plotlines, but also because New York itself is such a challenge. Like the song says, if you can make it in New York, you can make it anywhere. New York University was chosen as the perfect college, since it was right in the middle of downtown, close to everything. Alas, NYU didn't want to cooperate.

Easy solution: call the place the University of New York!

The solution for casting seemed less easy.

Then Keri Russell auditioned.

Although she had to wait two hours and a dozen actresses before she got her shot, she put in an amazing performance that literally shocked the creators of the show.

Since they had envisioned *Felicity* as a bright but shy sort, not necessarily pretty, and certainly not popular in high school, when Keri appeared they had a problem with her.

"She was so beautiful and such an angel," Abrams told James Collins of *Time*. "I thought there was no way she could be Felicity. But then she started reading, and she was funny as hell. She could be pretty and funny but also vulnerable."

You really can see this on the show. Although Keri Russell is luminous and wonderful, she is such a good actress that she can ACT plain and shy and unpopular.

The other applicants hadn't thought to make Felicity funny.

Keri got the job.

FELICITY'S FRIENDS

Finding the perfect best friend for Felicity was not anywhere near as difficult as finding Felicity herself. Amy Jo Johnson quickly got the part.

Finding the right guys for the roles of the Guy Who Felicity Chases—and the sweet Resident Adviser Who Talks Felicity into Staying took a while. But Scott Speedman and Scott Foley were found, and so all was ready. A pilot could be filmed.

Unfortunately, there was one major problem.

Since the pilot had to be absolutely perfect, so did the name of the guy who Felicity chases to New York.

And they hadn't named him yet.

Right in the middle of the shooting of the pilot, Keri went to Abrams and asked him the guy's name, since she had a scene with him that day.

Understand, there had been months of hair-pulling and sweating on the subject.

Pinned down, Abrams and Reeves picked ''Ben''—and were stuck with the name forever.

PILOT

Felicity had not always been scheduled for Tuesday night.

In fact, there was a great deal of fuss and bother about exactly where to put it!

TV programming is a science, but an extraordinary amount of it simply doesn't work well.

However, when it does work, it works great.

Let me give you an example:

Remember *Seinfeld*?

Sure, how could you forget? It's barely into reruns! Well, *Seinfeld* inherited a prime spot in NBC's lineup, namely Thursday night at nine P.M., from *Cheers*. For years *Cheers* was a big hit in that time slot. What NBC did with *Cheers* and *Seinfeld* was to count on viewers tuning in earlier or staying on after their favorite show, right in the midst of prime-time entertainment. A good case could be made for *ER*'s immense popularity stemming from its position right after *Seinfeld*.

So, when Bugs and Daffy at The WB . . . er, I mean, the brilliant programmers there decided that *Dawson's Creek* was a strong enough show to draw viewers to another night, a spot opened up in The WB's entertainment list.

The spot that had gotten so many people to watch *Dawson's Creek*: nine P.M. to ten P.M., right after *Buffy the Vampire Slayer*.

The "suits" (that's what the executives are called in Hollywoodspeak, since they tend to wear ties and coats, while producers, directors, and writers wear more casual attire) . . . er . . . the head folk at The WB were so happy with the potential of the pilot after it was filmed that WB network

CEO Jamie Kellner decided that it should get the spot right after *Buffy*.

"I'm down with that," Abrams said at the time, according to *Entertainment Weekly*. "We'll just add a little karate."

However, the decision was not final.

After the full pilot was finished (the producers started out with a shorter pilot to let folks see what they had), there was another meeting.

It was here that another important decision was made. Everyone had loved the final pilot, but the question of where it would be placed on the schedule had not been quite resolved at that time.

Lots of possibilities were tried all over the week, but finally everyone realized that Tony Krantz, one of the executive producers of *Felicity,* was right.

It should go in the best slot: nine to ten P.M., Tuesday night, right after *Buffy the Vampire Slayer*.

Not only that, but a nice number of episodes were planned. *Felicity* would have at least thirteen shows filmed to try to gain the audience that The WB wanted.

IRISH MAGIC

Keri Russell was filming *Mad About Mambo* in Ireland when The WB's fall schedule was to be announced in New York City.

The WB wanted her to be there to meet with advertisers and press.

Unfortunately, the director of *Mad About Mambo* pointed out that Keri really should stick around and do her work on the film.

Keri told him how important this meeting was, but the director was firm.

No, he said. You have to stay here.

Then Keri cried.

Can you imagine not having your heart melted by the sight of Keri Russell crying? The director relented, gave her a few days off, and managed to "film around her" (that is, do scenes in which Keri's character was not featured).

Keri flew to New York, where she was a smash hit with all the folks who met her. Everyone loved the pilot, and if anything, they loved Keri even more. Many thought that she would be the star of the new season . . . not just on The WB, but on all the networks.

When it was announced that *Felicity* had been placed in the slot after *Buffy*, there was cheering.

Keri Russell—and *Felicity*—had won them over.

CHARMING BARNSTORMER

If you were a critic for a newspaper or a TV station—or heck, now maybe even a popular Web site, every year you'd go to Los Angeles for the annual press tour.

Here the critics get a chance to see the new shows that are slated for the following season. This is not just so they can write or talk about the shows, and get advance word going—it's so they can write about the stars of the shows and get the chance to ask the questions that will provide the information they need to put into their pieces.

After seeing what all six networks had to offer, there was one hands-down favorite.

Felicity.

When the other network heads asked what show they wished was in their lineup, they all named one show.

Felicity.

The critics and reporters loved Keri and the other actors, and they were so enthusiastic about the show, they did not ask difficult questions. However, they did note the similarites between *Felicity* and *Ally McBeal.*

The creators just smiled and explained the story—just as I've explained it here.

Besides. There's no animated dancing baby on *Felicity,* right?

thirteen

The Producers

In the TV industry in Hollywood, you can't just fly in from your job as a computer salesman in Austin, Texas, and give a network a great idea, which they immediately buy and put on the air for you.

No. You have to have a past in the business.

You have to have credentials and connections.

In the case of the team that put together the show *Felicity* and now run it, all you can say is:

Wow! What great credentials!

THE GUY WITH THE IDEA

It was J. J., of course, who knew a girl named Felicity in his high school. He hasn't heard from her in a few years—but now he knows a new Felicity, who is very close to him . . . our Felicity.

J. J. Abrams, that is.

J. J. is the guy who dreamed up the notion of the whole *Felicity* plot off during his honeymoon a few years ago, remember?

Anyway, here's a little bit about J. J. you might like to know:

Although he was born in New York about thirty-two years ago, he was mostly raised in Los Angeles, which explains part of why he fits into the entertainment scene so well there.

Another reason is what happened to him when he was eight.

At that age, his grandfather took him on the Universal Studios tour. J. J. was so thrilled by the idea of making movies that he pestered his family until they bought him a Super 8 film camera. Immediately, J. J. set to work, filming and filming, and then editing his work into short subjects. When he learned that there were people other than his friends and family he could show these films to, he set out to do just that. J. J. entered his work into amateur film contests.

He started winning awards!

It was during one of these contests that he met someone who was to become a very significant part of his life. This was none other than cocreator of *Felicity,* Matt Reeves. Of course, they didn't immediately look at each other and say, "Let's do a series for The WB!" There were only three networks at that time, not six, like today.

No, they probably talked about Godzilla movies and what batteries lasted the longest.

Anyway, J. J. kept in touch with Matt all the way through college. Like Felicity, he decided to leave the West Coast for the East Coast in order to go to college in New York. He attended—and graduated from—Sarah Lawrence College in Bronxville, New York.

In the last year of college, J. J. teamed up with a friend to write a film treatment. After college the treatment sold and eventually became a movie starring Charles Grodin and James Belushi called *Taking Care of Business*.

This was an auspicious start.

J. J. was back in Los Angeles at this time, of course, with a feature-film credit.

He worked hard as a writer.

When you write films, you have to be good at creating scripts, but you also have to be good in talking to other people about ideas and finding out what production company wants what. Most often, when a script is written and "optioned" (leased) or bought, it gets a lot of feedback from producers and story people, so it changes a lot. Many, many scripts that have been written and paid for never get produced. We can probably assume that J. J. had a few of those.

However, he continued onward with writing scripts that were produced. His next produced film was *Regarding Henry* starring Harrison Ford. After that, he did *Forever Young* with Mel Gibson.

He also worked on an independent film with Jennifer Love Hewitt and Ben Stiller called *The Suburbans*. As an actor, you can spot J. J. in the features *Diabolique* and *Six Degrees of Separation*.

These, of course, are available in your local video store. If you haven't seen them yet, you should. They're good movies.

A blockbuster film of J. J.'s that hit the screens last summer and is available now for rental is the famous *Armageddon* with Bruce Willis. New York City doesn't get a cute, curly-haired new coed for that one. It gets destroyed!

Although J. J. got his start producing and directing amateur films, only recently has he been producing and directing professional films.

One of the many reasons that J. J. came to Matt with the *Felicity* idea was that they were already working on a film. That was *The Pallbearer,* for which J. J. got a producer credit.

He's also doing his very first TV directing job, calling the shots for an episode of *Felicity*.

Of course, just because he's in TV now doesn't mean that he's left his film work behind. In fact, J. J. has an upcoming movie that he cowrote. It's a thriller called *Squelch* and it was done by Twentieth Century-Fox.

Remember where J. J. conceived the idea for *Felicity*?

That's right. In the romantic South Seas, on his honeymoon.

I'm happy to report that there's another little guy around now who'll probably want some sort of camera soon.

When J. J. and his wife and small son aren't living in L.A., they're in New York.

Sounds like the cast of *Felicity*!

THE ONE WITH THE STYLE

If J. J. Abrams had the brainstorm, then Matt Reeves had the special touch needed to make it so lifelike.

Felicity's cocreator in some ways lived a parallel life to his collaborator. Both are about the same age. Both were born in New York (Rockville Centre, in Matt's case) and both grew up in Los Angeles. Both started making films at the age of eight, and both met an important person at age thirteen . . . each other.

They would call each other and keep in touch, comparing notes throughout their early youth. However, instead of heading east for college, Matt stuck around the L.A. area and went to the University of Southern California. This was important, since he attended the film school there—and the USC film school gave birth to many of our brightest film talents, including George Lucas and Francis Ford Coppola.

One of Matt's several short film school projects, "Mr. Petrified Forest" was so well done that it won him an agent as soon as he graduated. That agent, in turn, got him work.

One of Matt's first projects was a film script that he wrote with a friend. This was an action film that eventually was turned into *Under Siege II: Dark Territory* with Steven Seagal.

Matt's no stranger to TV.

He's done a lot of TV, including episodes of *Relativity* and *Homocide: Life on the Street.*

His first feature-film directing effort is of special interest to *Felicity* fans, I think.

THE PALLBEARER

Any fan of the show *Felicity* will want to head immediately to the video store and rent this film.

Why?

Because this movie, written and directed by one half of the team that created the series, has many of the same elements—and virtues—of the series.

Starring David Schwimmer, the mournful-looking guy on *Friends,* as a mournful-looking guy, it even starts out with the same slightly drifting credits.

Schwimmer plays twenty-five-year-old Tom, who lives with his mom (Carol Kane) in Brooklyn and is looking for an architectural job. When his old high-school crush, Julie (Gwyneth Paltrow) comes back to town, his friends think he should ask her out.

However, when a high-school classmate whom no one remembers kills himself, the grief-stricken mother (Barbara Hershey) mistakenly thinks that Tom was her son's best friend, and asks him to be a pallbearer and give the eulogy at the funeral—and then leans on him for other kind of support. This complication interferes with Tom's pursuit of Julie.

There are many elements that are striking about *The Pallbearer* when compared with *Felicity*, but perhaps the main one is the theme of people in transition—and the theme of having the courage to let go and move on in one's life.

Just as Felicity has to let go of her high-school feelings for Ben, so the characters in *The Pallbearer* have to move on from stuck periods in their lives. At the end of the film, Tom lets Julie go on with her life—but has the courage to move out of his mother's house and face the world.

Another interesting thing about *The Pallbearer* is that it's obvious who gave *Felicity* the look it has. Matt Reeves's directorial style is here—sharp and good-looking and thoughtful. His way with actors is also very much in evidence and there are deeply emotional moments in *The Pallbearer*, just as there are many funny elements. You can almost see *Felicity* in the making.

Another important similarity is that *The Pall-*

bearer is just full of life's excruciatingly embarrassing moments. For example, when Tom tries to kiss Julie, they bump heads. When Julie comes to visit him, his mother insists on calling him "Tom-Tom" and talking about the magic tricks he performed at age eight. After watching *The Pallbearer,* you have to think that it was Matt Reeves who came up with the part in *Felicity* where the deejay mistakenly plays Felicity's tape to Sally at a party, or the moment when Felicity throws up on Noel.

Most of all, *The Pallbearer* shows a definitely cinematic—that is, movie style—which comes through in *Felicity.*

Many TV shows are shot quickly and from very few angles. It's clear that *Felicity* takes time and thought with its shots and its acting.

So if there's one film that you should see if you're dying to see something else by one of *Felicity*'s creators . . .

I'd vote for *The Pallbearer.*

IN MATT'S CRYSTAL BALL

Coming up for Matt Reeves is a feature he cowrote, *The Yards,* which was produced by Miramax Films. James Gray directed, and the film features James Caan and Mark Wahlberg.

Unlike his cocreator, Matt just hangs around in Los Angeles most of the time.

OPIE IN CHARGE

Ever see the little kid in *The Andy Griffith Show*? And the teenager in *Happy Days*.

If you have, maybe you've been watching too much TV!

Seriously, one of the things you'll notice in the Los Angeles entertainment scene is that as soon as a star or director gets famous, he or she forms a production company! A good example of this is Steven Spielberg, who created Amblin Entertainment. These companies develop TV and film projects and work with the bigger studios to create the entertainment for movies and TV.

It wasn't his role as Opie in *Andy Griffith* or his stint on *Happy Days* that made Ron Howard a true star, though. It was his work as a film director.

Ron was born in Duncan, Oklahoma, and made his first screen appearance in the film *The Journey* at the age of four.

From the time he was a kid, Ron had always been interested in things on the other side of the camera.

Ron Howard's first big film as a director was *Cocoon*.

After that he formed Imagine Entertainment with Brian Grazer and Tony Krantz and has directed some of Imagine's features, including *Ransom* and *Apollo 13,* and *Liar, Liar* and *The Nutty Professor.*

Felicity is a production of Imagine Entertainment

and Ron is one of the executive producers of the show.

Pretty soon Ron's next film, *Ed TV,* will be out, with Woody Harrelson.

Sometimes Ron still acts. Let's hope he shows up in an episode of *Felicity*!

AGENT AND PRODUCER

The final two of the executive producers of *Felicity* are Tony Krantz and Brian Grazer. Both are co-owners of Imagine Entertainment.

Tony Krantz, unlike the others, got his start with the famous CAA agency. That stands for Creative Artists Agency, in case you wondered. Tony had been to college at the University of California, Berkeley, and slipped easily into the L.A. scene.

Quite often, big agencies like CAA "package" shows. In other words, they put together concepts with writers, directors, and producers and attach big stars to these.

Shows that Tony Krantz packaged in his day have been *ER, Twin Peaks, Melrose Place,* and *Beverly Hills 90210.*

The other illustrious partner of Imagine Entertainment and executive producer for *Felicity* is Brian Grazer. He's also an executive producer, like the others, for *The PJs,* a TV show coming up on the Fox Network featuring the voice of Eddie Murphy, and *Sports Night* on ABC.

Brian also produced *The 'Burbs* with Tom Hanks.

These guys are important parts of *Felicity*, helping to guide it through all the difficult spots toward broadcast.

There are also lots and lots of other people who are important in putting the show on the air. The TV industry has many, many unsung heroes.

You can check out their names on the credits in front of and after the show.

Do it! You'll see these terrific talents around for a long time to come!

fourteen

But What Are People Saying?

THE BIG BUZZ

Felicity was a show that was a success before it even hit the airwaves.

Long before the September 29, 1998, airdate, Keri's picture was gracing covers of magazines, Web sites, and stories about her were appearing in newspapers and magazines.

It's true that Keri's charm and looks helped launch this frenzy, this excited buzz. But savvy and intelligent advance publicity on the part of under-dog WB had a lot going for it. The WB, until as recently as a year before, had been marked for doom. In a universe of cable channels, the Internet, and too many networks, it seemed to have the least chance of survival.

Then *Buffy* staked out her territory.

Buffy the Vampire Slayer, that is, the surprise hit that mixed spiffy campy horror with high-school heartthrobs. The chemistry clicked, and the magic raised *Dawson's Creek* from the grave.

Smart programmers moved *Buffy* to Tuesday nights at eight, making it a perfect lead-in to create a new hit. That hit proved to be a monster hit—though a much more pleasant monster than any battled by Buffy.

Dawson's Creek took the country by storm, combining bright, sassy dialogue with raw sexy character appeal. Created and written by the creator of *Scream* and *Scream II,* Kevin Williamson, *Dawson's Creek* introduced the delightful and deep teen characters of Dawson, his best bud Pacey, and romantic interests Joey and Jen. The actors who played them, James Van Der Beek, Josh Jackson, Katie Holmes, and Michelle Williams became stars.

Having created a bigger hit than they could have hoped for, The WB masters realized that by moving *Dawson's Creek* to Wednesday at eight, the nine o'clock slot for that night could introduce another possible hit. That hit proved to be *Charmed,* with the bewitching Shannen Doherty and other teen faves.

But what about Tuesday night?

Lots of attention was paid to the nine o'clock

slot on that night. A project, fortunately, was already in the works—a show that ABC had rejected, but that had all the key ingredients that *Dawson* had, only with a few more relevant ones to boot.

This, of course, was our *Felicity*.

Once the pilot was filmed, it was not only picked up for a half season of shows, it was shown to prospective advertisers, who went bananas. Not stupid people, advertisers saw that this show was not only a golden hit—it had all the elements that would make it popular among just the people they wanted to reach.

You!

Not only that, it was a deep show that didn't patronize or underestimate its audience's intelligence. It was about real people with real problems.

When The WB sent out its initial press kits to reviewers, there was already a large number of raves for the show. . . . Yet it had not actually been reviewed in any of the media. No, the excited reviews were from advertisers who had lined up for the chance to place their commercials on *Felicity*.

Nonetheless, The WB wasn't worried.

They knew that they had something special.

And when the reviews hit the open air, The WB proved not only that they were right, but that they weren't going to be the number-five network much longer!

AND THE VERDICT IS . . .

"There's no doubting that *Felicity* will be a hit," reported *Mr. Showbiz* on the Web after viewing the first episode.

"It's [Keri] Russell, twenty-two, who gives *Felicity* its magnetism," said the *San Francisco Chronicle*. "*Felicity* is the prime cause of envy on network executive rows this fall."

In a feature spot along with two other related articles, *USA Today* gave *Felicity* three out of four stars. "For those who follow romances, this is the *Dirty Dancing* fantasy in another guise: the smart good girl who falls for a not-so-bright bad boy. It seldom works out well in real life, but that doesn't make the fantasy any less powerful," notes reviewer Robert Bianco. "This clever coming-of-age drama is not just about romance—and the lead character is not some anti-feminist nightmare who has sacrificed her life for love. Felicity has chosen to change her life, and that's a pretty scary decision at any age."

Rolling Stone called *Felicity* "exceptionally well-shot and performed."

Noting that "WB's *Felicity* is one of the most promising series of the fall," *L.A. Times* TV critic Howard Rosenberg wrote, "Felicity and her friends seem right on the mark . . . " And "this appealingly romantic series whose likable heroine [is] played all fresh and whipped creamy by the luminous [Keri] Russell.''

The often grumpy Tom Shales (one of my favorite critics) called *Felicity* ''the best new drama of the season so far,'' in the *Washington Post*. He goes on to say that ''*Felicity* is so skillfully written and acted that it's hard to imagine an age group that couldn't be touched by it and feel involved.''

People magazine opines: ''[Keri] Russell has an unassuming sort of star quality that draws us to her character, and the writing in the pilot is sensitive without being soapy. Bottom Line: Promising Freshman.''

Entertainment Weekly, in its October 2, 1998, issue states: ''Felicity would be a lot more difficult to bear were Russell not so committed to her gushiness—alert and registering every emotion on her face, she has none of the affectless cool that makes the *Party of Five* clan such poker-face pains. And [the producers] keep the story from bogging down with briskly paced scenes and vivid characterization. If Felicity doesn't quite live up to its hype as the season's niftiest new show, it's on its way to being a solid weekly soap opera.''

Now you can understand why magazines like *Entertainment Weekly* and *People* joined the bandwagon. That's their job. But when a high-brow magazine like *The New Yorker* takes notice of a new TV drama-comedy—wow! You know something very interesting is up!

"*Felicity* has been touted as this year's *Dawson's Creek*," says essayist Nancy Franklin. "In addition to featuring sweet-faced young men who have thoughtful hair, the shows share a muffled, draggy quality. The kids in these teen-noir series all have a slightly swollen look, as if they'd had an allergic reaction to life and they are in dead earnest—you search their faces in vain for a sign of an interestingly wicked, inappropriate, funny thought."

Those grown-ups! They just don't understand sometimes!

In the *New York Times,* Caryn James says, "The one series to be preordained a hit by advertisers and critics, *Felicity* piles on the ingredients of success so deftly it is likely to join The WB's list of hit teen-age oriented shows."

Of course, these are all reviews of the first show—the pilot that started the *Felicity* buzz in the first place.

What about the rest of the shows?

This viewer is happy to report that the quality of the pilot is maintained throughout the later episodes, which is why *Felicity* remains extremely worth watching.

The second show, in which Felicity deals with her parents and reaffirms her decision to remain in New York City, was perhaps a little slow, and the new characters that have helped so much (like tangy Tangi Miller as Elena) and the plotlines (Julie's friendship with the shy film student in the pink underwear) perhaps could have been put into motion sooner.

Apparently, other viewers felt this way, too, as the show's ratings cooled somewhat after the second episode.

However, they've started climbing again, and no wonder.

Felicity is absolutely unique.

For one thing, the filming is movie quality, which is no wonder, since *Felicity* often uses theatrical-film directors like Matt Reeves and Joan Tewkesbury. Each frame is artful and considered.

True, college isn't quite like what's depicted as being in *Felicity*. And the show's portrayal of New York isn't quite accurate. But then, it's extremely good for a TV series that's actually filmed mostly in Los Angeles!

What I like the most about the series (besides the remarkable and endearing Keri Russell, of course) is the way it gives the characters time to breathe. You don't get the feeling that the plot is trying to hurry the show along. The characters have enough time and space to seem real. And if coincidences seem to occur from time to time . . . well, they happen in real life, too. In any case, the stories are not contrived or forced, and although you could call this a ''soap opera'' in that it has a continuing story line like the daytime soaps, it doesn't rely on cliffhangers and melodrama like those stories do.

It's trying to deal with real life.

One review on the Web pointed out early on what *Felicity*'s promise was: a forum to deal with issues of teens and early twentysomethings in a difficult and confusing world.

I think that all the episodes of *Felicity* are doing that, and in an unusual, low-key, and feeling kind of way.

FELICITY 2000

Will Felicity become more emotionally involved with Ben?

Will Noel break up his long-distance relationship and successfully court our heroine?

Just what courses will the story line take?

Well, of course, that's being kept a secret. You can bet that Felicity and her two male friends will continue yo-yoing back and forth, and you know there will be entanglements and misunderstandings.

My guess, though, is that while Ben and Noel will remain as main characters throughout the show's run, Felicity will meet someone else special.

Not only is the series set at a university, filled with guys, but that university is in the middle of New York City—also filled with guys. With Felicity serving coffee at Dean and Deluca, can it be long before some handsome well-mannered professional notices her charm and asks her out?

Like that old TV series used to say, there are eight million stories in New York City.

You can bet that *Felicity*'s writers will be able to bring in anything they want.

Here are my predictions:

¤ *There will be more minorities on the show.*

Why? Because New York is just filled with people from all over the world.

¤ *There will be gay men on the show, and Felicity will probably befriend at least one.*

Why? Again, New York is a diverse city and has a large gay/bisexual population.

¤ *Felicity or its characters will have interactions with the showbiz world in New York.*

With Broadway and Off-Broadway so close by, how can the writers keep these elements out? And we're already seeing Ben heading in that direction with that drama class that's actually tapping hidden talents.

¤ *Felicity will change majors.*

The choice of careers for a college student is a prime source of anguish and hand-wringing. Felicity is one bright girl. As she becomes more independent and aware of other potential careers, she'll realize that she doesn't have to be a doctor. This will, of course, cause more friction with her family.

◘ *Felicity will get a boyfriend.*

Noel? Ben? Neither, I think.

The series needs another magnetic male character along the lines of Dawson in *Dawson's Creek*. Felicity will fall for this character and then go through the difficult decision of how far to take their relationship. Will she have sex with this new guy? Noel and Ben will be there to comfort and advise her—and be green with envy.

The more one considers the possibilities presented by the premise of the show, the more excited a fan becomes.

There are all kinds of stories possible.

Best of all, you can count on one thing with *Felicity*.

You can expect the unexpected!

fifteen

Sally

MYSTERY

Who is Sally?

Each episode of *Felicity* uses a clever device to get inside its heroine's thoughts.

There are voice-overs—that is, an unseen person speaking over the action shown on the screen by the main character, Felicity. Usually, these just happen. It's like when Ben tells his English teachers what "soliloquies" are in *Hamlet*. They are the characters speaking directly to the audience.

In *Felicity*, though, Keri Russell as Felicity trades tapes with a close friend, talking about her feelings and telling her what is happening in her life.

This narrative tool allows the writers and directors to play with time and place, showing how creative and brilliant and innovative these folk are.

It also allows another character to comment on the proceedings. This is "Sally Reardon," who sends Felicity her tapes.

But again, *who* is Sally?

Well, we know that Sally was Felicity's French tutor in high school and we get to hear about Sally's life as well. She's a twenty- or thirty-something woman. She gives Felicity advice and seems warm and caring—but sometimes a little sardonic.

Yes, but we never see Sally. Whose voice is that?

It's a mystery that has been discussed a great deal on *Felicity* newsgroups.

"Legally, all we're allowed to say," disclosed J. J. Abrams on an *E! Online* chat, "is that we have a mysterious, unnamed superstar playing that voice."

It's a very familiar-sounding voice.

Hmm. Well, after all, it *is* Warner Brothers we're dealing with here.

Could it be the voice guy for Bugs and Daffy?

No, not the famous Mel Blanc. He died a few years ago and they've got people now who can imitate him doing Bugs Bunny and Daffy Duck.

Meryl Streep?

No. The voice is deeper than Meryl's.

Cher? Cher has a deep voice.

No. Probably not. They would probably want someone who would be well known by a younger set.

In any case, again the use of the voice and the mystery behind it is another case of brilliance on the part of the producers. There hasn't been anything quite like it since Whoopi Goldberg made semiregular appearances as Guinan on *Star Trek: The Next Generation* in a rather similar role.

Is Sally voiced by Whoopi?

Next time you watch *Felicity,* I suggest that you listen to the voice of Sally very carefully.

And make your guess!

SIXTEEN

Scandal!

POSE

"It blew my mind!" creator/producer J. J. Abrams told a chatroom audience on *E! Online* when asked about the scandal. "We all treated her like she was nineteen!"

Abrams was referring to the news that broke on *Entertainment Weekly* about Riley Weston, one of the writers.

Riley Weston was not her real name. It was really Kimberlee Kramer and the scandal was about her age. Rather than being underage, though, she'd been "overage" . . .

Or so the story went.

In her pose, Riley claimed to be nineteen years old, which made her look like a writer wonder.

It's very unusual for a person so young to have

developed the kind of skills necessary to write television scripts.

How and why did this happen?

The story broke on *Entertainment Tonight* on Thursday, October 15. *ET* had just done a story in which they interviewed Riley, who had a part on the episode that was to air on Tuesday, November 17. Riley had also cowritten that episode.

She'd also just signed a writing contract with Disney, the parent company of Touchstone, who owns the show *Felicity,* worth almost half a million dollars.

Then the entertainment news show got a tip. This was the same woman, said the tip, the same actress who had appeared in *Sister Act II* as "Kimberlee Kramer." *ET* checked. Sure enough, both Kimberlee and Riley had the same social security number.

When *ET* called Riley Weston, she agreed to do an interview on the show, and explain.

"This is obviously a huge apology," she said, admitting the hoax she had perpetrated.

Did she regret it?

"Yes, I regret it," she told *Entertainment Tonight.* "At the same time, I knew no other way around it because all I wanted to get was a job."

The perky, impish Riley, a brunette, obviously does look younger than her thirty-two years. And when asked about the writing work that got her the script jobs, she insists that they are "absolutely 100 percent my writing. That is the bottom line."

Why was it necessary to lie? She could act and she could write. Why did she have to change her name and lie about her age?

It's difficult to understand outside the city, but in the show-business world of Hollywood, youth is a highly valuable commodity. The common assumption is that younger is better and that the talented young are the best.

Apparently, Kimberlee Kramer could not get past the age bias in the business, so she fell back on the fact that she actually looked young—and had talent.

"I did it as an actor first," she explained.

But then when she showed her writing, there was no way that she could explain that she was really thirty-two years old.

J. J. Abrams admitted (not on *ET*) that he hired Riley for the script work for two reasons. Because she could obviously write well, and because she was nineteen. He felt that having a true nineteen-year-old on staff would help portray that state of mind on the show with more honesty and truth.

Other Hollywood folk were quick to condemn all forms of age bias and claim their freedom from it, crowing about their older writers—but you can sympathize with J. J., truly.

After all, you could understand why J. J. wouldn't want to hire, say, Meryl Streep to play Felicity, even though she's one of the finest actresses alive. She just doesn't look young enough. People wouldn't believe her in the role.

When Imagine Entertainment, the people who produce *Felicity,* heard about the truth, they issued a statement:

"The recent accusations concerning Riley's background are a complete surprise to all of us. We trusted her as a colleague and are saddened by the dishonesty. Whatever explanations there are for her behavior ultimately rest with Riley herself."

"These are unbelievably wonderful people," Riley assured *ET.* "I feel terrible to have done that to them."

Entertainment Weekly was a little more amused.

After all, they'd been caught in the hoax as well, naming Riley as one of the hundred most creative people in Hollywood in their "IT" issue last June.

They, too, had a talk with Riley and she was more than happy to be obliged to apologize—but also to point out, "It came down to working as an actor. Show me an actor who's never lied about their age."

Too true. Some of the people in this book seem to have shifting ages in different reports, I've noticed.

According to *Entertainment Weekly*'s October 30 issue, Riley got the job on *Felicity* when her agency, United Talent, showed them a script she'd written about teenage sisters. Riley then claimed to be eighteen. She put up a *Titanic* poster on her office wall and claimed to be smitten with Jonathan Taylor Thomas.

Apparently some folks thought she was very like Felicity.

She was a story person for seven *Felicity* scripts (suggesting situations and dialogue in meetings). The one script for which she gets cocredit was aired on November 17; she also guest-starred as a teen named Story in the episode.

In the October 25, 1998, issue of the *Chicago Tribune,* Riley is quoted as saying, "If you were getting a job in any other industry, do you think that anyone would care how old I am or how I look?"

She also pointed out, "I did what I had to to succeed."

Tribune writer Gary Dretzka reported: "Those of us covering Hollywood know that Weston certainly isn't alone in her anxiety over industry ageism. In the last six months alone, this reporter was given the brush-off four separate times when inquiries were made about birthdays (when pressed, one publicist played the Jack Benny card by making her late fortyish client thirty-nine.)"

The news of this scandal even made a paper as far away as London, England.

In the Sunday *Times* of October 25, 1998, the delightful columnist Zoë Heller writes:

"It's not at all clear to me why pretending to be younger than you are is more morally reprehensible when you're trying to be a writer than when you're trying to be a television babe. In both cases, the burden of moral embarrassment is not on the pretender, but on the system that fetishizes youth. The Weston case is salutary in so far as it points up the fact that all workers in the Hollywod system—even writers, who you might reasonably expect to be prized for their experience—feel the pressure of youth-mania. Over the years, I have met no fewer than five male writers who tinted their hair in order that their greying temples would not repulse whizkid studio executives. One female writer I know has been twenty-nine for at least half a decade."

The crew of *Felicity* liked Riley enough to give her a nineteenth-birthday party. She left the show not because she was fired, but because her option was up and Disney had signed her to that development deal.

Certainly J. J. Abrams isn't mad.

"I wish her all the best," the thirty-two-going-on-thirty-three-year-old creator/producer declared on *E! Online*.

No harm done. Publicity for *Felicity*, certainly.

But it does show that if you want to make it in Hollywood and you're young . . .

Learn to write!

seventeen

Touring the Web with *Felicity*

INFO, INFO, INFO!

One of the great things about now is the World Wide Web.

Thanks to the ingenious use of the Internet, Web sites have been developed. Using HTML (Hyper Text Markup Language) Webmasters can create their own sites for people to visit (with the magical help of a computer, their computer's modem, and a communications server).

Anyone with the desire (and a small amount of money) can set up their own Web sites about themselves or whatever they want. The result has been sites about just about anything and everything, and sites set up by fans to celebrate their loves, and to help give information and interact with fellow fans.

This has certainly been the case with *Felicity*.

Even before the show began to air, there were Web sites to help people see what was emerging from The WB. Even before *Felicity,* though, there were Web sites about two of its stars, Keri Russell and Amy Jo Johnson, because of their previous work.

Why should you be interested in this?

Well, because all of these Web sites change. By the time you've read this book, the sites mentioned in it will have new stuff, new information, and new fun available to you.

But you need to know where to go first.

If you don't have a computer, your neighborhood library might have one you can surf the Web with—or your school certainly should.

Here's a little bit of help to get you going and some signposts along your journey.

THE KERI RUSSELL WEBPAGE

Here's my favorite site about Keri Russell. Astonishingly enough, it's done in Finland. Yes, Finland—the Scandinavian country between Sweden and Russia.

Apparently, the Webmaster who started it—a fellow by the name of Oskari "Okko" Ojala—has been a Keri Russell fan for a long time and has been working a long time to get other people interested in her.

The site is filled with great pictures of Keri, but it's got lots of text as well. Bio, chats, filmography—and a great "links" page. (Links take you to other sites that concern the subject.)

As of the last dip in the surf, Niklas "Xanthic" Westershatrahle had taken over the pages, since Okko had less time to take care of them because of military duties. He was also discouraged because Keri (rumored to have a laptop and an E-mail account somewhere) had never E-mailed him a message, although he'd announced that he would really enjoy one. (The problem with E-mailing, though, is that you have to give away your E-mail address, which Keri probably doesn't want to do.) He'd also hoped that the site would be the "official" Keri Russell site—that is, approved by her. Alas, this never happened.

The site is now: http://www.sci.fi/~Xanthic/keri

Thanks for setting up a great site, Okko!

THE BEST FOR AMY JO

Fans certainly are dedicated.

No one seems to have a more dedicated fan than Amy Jo Johnson. The president of the "Amy Jo Johnson Fan Club," Roxanne Nolan, has created a terrific WebPage dedicated to her idol, with lots of answers to questions, pictures, information about Amy Jo's movies and TV series . . . and extra treats.

If you want to find out the absolute latest on Amy Jo, the best place to go is here:
http://www.amyjojohnson/net.

THE WWW WEB SITES

If you've got access to a really good computer arrangement, you should definitely head to a couple of impressive sites.

The first stop on the suggested list is:
http://www.tvplex.com/touchstone/felicity

This is a site owned and operated by Buena Vista, and if you've been watching your credits, you recognize the name. Yep, Buena Vista is the Walt Disney Company. Since the Walt Disney Company also owns Touchstone, the production company for *Felicity* . . . well, you get the idea.

Actually, this is a site done by TV PLEX and it's a pretty astonishing one. You need to download a special process called MicroMedia Flash, but if you can do this, what you get are some beautiful graphics and a nice presentation with bells and whistles and a lovely picture of Keri Russell to start your way. (If you don't have Flash tech, you can click on another button so you can view the site normally.) What you'll get is a well-thought-out selection consisting of the following subjects: "About the Show," "About the Cast," a nice "Photo Album," a "Behind the Scenes" section, a "Keepers" section—and finally a place where you can write your comments on the show.

This is one of nicest Web sites I've ever seen—and you should keep on checking it out to see how TV PLEX updates it.

While you're there, you ought to check out the rest of TV PLEX, too!

You don't even have to type the next official site into your browser. The TV PLEX site has a button that will zip you instantly there.

This one is appropriately titled felicity.com, so even if you're not going through TV PLEX, you can get there easily by just typing into your destination box:

http://felicity.com

This one didn't pop up in the World Wide Web universe until a few weeks after the debut of the show, and it's constantly getting additions, so it's one you'll want to bookmark and come back to often.

It's the full Touchstone site and you can tell these people are on the inside because there are always intriguing hints into what's going to happen in coming weeks. Additionally, there are also super graphics, really excellent pictures you can't get anywhere else—and snappy write-ups about cast, crew, and producers.

Best of all, this is a great place to give the people in charge of the show your feedback. Thanks to a special form, you can E-mail the producers about what you think. Not only your thoughts about individual episodes but about themes on the show. Often these remarks are posted, so you can read the thoughts of your fellow *Felicity* viewers.

If you want, you can head onward to what The WB has posted about *Felicity* on its site (http://thewb.com). But face it, the best stuff is straight from the source at those other wonderful Web sites.

FUNNY AND FUN *FELICITY*

If you think that *Felicity* gets a little too serious at times, then a great antidote might be a Web site called *Will Felicity Cry?* (http://www.geo.cities.com/SouthBeach/Docks/8927).

Here visitors can try to predict how many times Felicity cries in upcoming episodes. (Things do get a little weepy there at times, don't they?)

On the other hand, if you just want to have some *Felicity* fun, you can go to *All Felicity* (http://fly.to/felicity). Lots of pictures and information here. Plus, there's someone who loves the show so much they actually transcribe the scripts and post them on the Web! So if you miss choice bits of dialogue and didn't tape the show, you can just go here and read.

Best of all, on the *All Felicity* page, you can sign

up for a special *Felicity* newsletter. Every once in a while afterward, you'll find a jolly little bit of E-mail, consisting of *Felicity* facts, quotes, and delicious details from the show—including quizzes to let you see how much attention you've been paying!

ALL UNOFFICIAL *FELICITY*

If you've been reading carefully, you'll know that *Felicity* started a lot of talk and interest long before it ever actually debuted on The WB.

· The first site to go up about the show that had nothing to do with anyone who actually owned rights to it was humorously named *The First Unofficial Felicity WebPage* and it was put together quite nicely by Lisa Jayne (http://www.geocities.com/SouthBeach/Inlet/3211/felicity.htm/).

Although there are plenty of other Felicity Web-Pages out there right now, all Felicity Websurfers should pay homage to this first one not just to do it honor, but to enjoy its contents.

Great contents they are, too!

For one thing, the site has a unique poll. Right there, you can vote on which character from the show you like best—Ben, Elena, Julie, Noel, or of course, Felicity herself.

What's more, you can cruise through nice write-ups about the cast and check out some terrific interviews. There's a nice summary of the episodes, a multimedia page, links galore, and even a guestbook to let Lisa know you appreciate her work and devotion to the cause.

One of those links will take you to another fine page, this one called *Fans of WB's Felicity*. (It's http://www.geocities. com/~fporter, if you're superimpatient.)

This one's got a nice piece called "Who Is Felicity?" and it's taking good care of the news and views on the show, as well as media reports—and yes—terrific pictures of all the cast members. Links and E-mail spots, too!

MORE FANS OF *FELICITY*

One-stop *Felicity* shopping?

You can't go wrong with this one!

At *Fans of Felicity* (http://www.angelfire.com/ny/fansoffelicity/index.html) hosted by someone named Aliey.

Here you've got a terrific "Seen and Heard" section with live video clips from the show, and live interviews as well. There are quotes and a picture gallery.

If anything, even better is *Felicity's World* at http://www.geocities.com/TelevisionCity/Stage/7055/Index.html.

You can choose "Frames" or "No Frames." Best would be "Frames" if your computer can handle it, because this gives you easy access to all the cool stuff here.

This is one of the hippest sites, since it keeps up-to-date on the show and all its controversies and surprises. It's the one site that kept up with the burning question: Would the Pink Guy turn out to be the Bad Guy?

Felicity's World's sections include a right-on description of the show, loads of pictures (natch!), the latest news, a quickly updated episode summary, cast and character descriptions, those naughty transcripts we told you about, neat quotes from the show, a music list of everything that's been played on *Felicity* . . . This one's even got an area in the "MISC." section where you can learn to dress like Felicity.

Talk about a complete fan site! Wow!

MORE! MORE!

Up next is another good site (http://ll.org/felicity/). It's called *The Felicity Fan Zone* and it has special allowances for which browser you use (like Netscape or Explorer). This one specializes in videos and pictures. And oh? You want to know what music was played on *Felicity* and exactly where to go on the Web to get it. Look no further. It's right here.

Last time we looked, the Webmaster was looking for someone to help maintain these pages. So if you're interested in getting involved not only with the world of *Felicity*, but in polishing up your HTML . . . search no further!

Up next: a curious site called *Felicity in New York*. It's at http://hometown.aol.com/pumbaa36/index.html. Feel like getting this Webmaster's favorite quotes? Or finding out exactly what Ben wrote in Felicity's yearbook? Well, this is the spot for that, a nice selection of photos and other thoughts about the show, plus a nice sampling of media articles.

Felicity for the Fans, at http://www.geocities.com/TelevisionCity/Stage/6001, has lots of what the other sites have (there are only so many pictures running around, after all!) but features a special "Coffee House Chat" to talk about the show and a "Forum" where you can state your opinion.

NO ONE'S BORED ON THIS BOARD

If that last bit sent thrills to your toes, you'll definitely want to visit http://www.InsideTheWeb.com/messageboard/mbs.cgi/mb167845. It's the *Felicity Discussion Board*. Here you can post your feelings and thoughts and experiences similar to those of these characters. There are strings of topics and also expressions of approval or disapproval of the show.

If this sort of thing just tickles you pink, you'll have to also check out the "official" message board. That would be the *Warner Brothers Message Board* at http://wbboards.warnerbros.com. Select "Felicity" and you're on your way! This one's hopping, and the nice thing is that you know that not only the head honchos of the show read the messages—maybe the stars lurk as well!

Finally, if you are a Keri Russell fan in particular, by all means post some message to the *Keri Russell Message Board.* That would be: http://www.kwfc.com/kerirussel/messageboard/msgboard.shtml

YET MORE

Another page to proudly proclaim its amateur status is *The Unofficial Felicity Web Site.* That's at http://members.tripod.com/~Amber_Soeurt/Index.html. It's got the usual slew of pictures and links, but there's some nice pictures here you may not have seen elsewhere.

Finally, at http://www.geocities.com/TelevisionCity/Studio/4928 you'll find the *Felicity Home Page.* What's special about this one is that along with the usual pictures, bios, and thoughts about the show, there's also an area where people can post their "FanFic" . . . that is, stories they've written themselves about *Felicity.*

Oh yes! Feeling a little overwhelmed by all these

site addresses? Well, there's at least one *Felicity* Web ring. (Web rings are Web sites that are members of a chain. You can go automatically from one to another. Just go to one of the unofficial sites. Chances are it's a part of the Web ring.)

Plus there's a *Felicity* Link Index at http://www.geocities.com/SouthBeach/Inlet/3211/felicity.html, where you'll find many of the above—and probably more by now!

THE VERY BEST FOR LAST

In the episode "Cheating," which aired on November 3, 1998, the character Noel Crane (played by Scott Foley) mentions that he's got a Web site to show off his budding graphic-design skill. He mentions that it's:

www.noelcrane.com

Some savvy and ingenious soul associated with the show actually went and created the sort of Web site that Noel might have. It's got great facts about *Felicity*'s dorms, pictures, tours of New York . . .

But enough. Go look for yourself.

You'll thank me!

eIGHteeN

The Best Bet for *Felicity* Fan Action

The *FELICITY* List

Can you say computer mailing list?

Okay, you can say it, but do you know what a computer mailing list is?

Well, basically it's a way that groups of people can stay in touch and post messages without having to go to a Web site or a special chat area on AOL or Compuserve.

Basically, its a chatroom right inside your E-mail box.

Felicity Fan, you are one of the lucky ones, because *Felicity* has a wonderful and very active computer mailing list.

A dedicated fan of the show named Alfredo Jacobo Perez Gomez has set up his computer as a robot to host this list, and boy, does it have some lively discussions.

To get on this mailing list, you can go to http://www.dreamworld.org/felicity and you'll get the scoop there.

However, if you can't get on the Web for some reason but you have E-mail, simply stated, what you have to do is this:

In your E-mail box, address your message to:
robot@dreamworld.org

In the body of the message write:
Join Felicity.

If you want to go off the list, just E-mail robot@dreamworld.org and type in the body of the mail:
Leave Felicity.

You can also get messages in a digest form, as well as get other options, but in my opinion, having new messages every day is more fun (although you have to make sure you erase them, or your box will get full!).

So what exactly goes on the *Felicity* mailing list? Lots!

TALKING, TALKING

One of the wonderful things about *Felicity* is how true-to-life it seems. It focuses on the small but vital problems that people face every day, and it deals with them honestly and thoughtfully. So, as a result, there's a lot that people can identify with. Not just teenagers and college students either, but older adults who still grapple with emotions and issues in their lives.

Lots of people on the mailing list point out these parts of *Felicity* and they say, "I can identify with that!" or "Something like that happened to me!" It's a great way to talk to other people about the feelings the show arouses in you, sort these feelings out . . . and help other people deal with their feelings.

Of course, this sounds dreadfully serious, and it's just a part of the list. Most significant, I think, is the immediate news you get concerning new articles about the series that are about to appear in magazines, what people have learned is coming up in future episodes, what cool new Web sites have sprung up . . .

One week, some people found out that both *Saturday Night Live* and *Mad TV* were going to present skits that Saturday evening that poked fun at *Felicity*. As a result, lots of people watched and then really enjoyed themselves talking about those skits.

Another virtue of the mailing list is that you get to make friends. Sometimes people who have common interests E-mail each other separately and find new friends. There's even a regular "extra" from the set of *Felicity* who's on the mailing list.

Lest you think this is much TOO serious, there's also lots of silliness, and amusing talking of bloopers and "Keepers." An example that includes both occurred when Julie was incorrectly operating a VCR remote control in a scene. A person noted the goof—and asked to be the "Keeper" of Julie's VCR remote control! (Fans like to "claim" inanimate objects on the show, believe it or not.)

Finally, you don't just talk about *Felicity*. Sometimes there are off-topic discussions that are brewed by things that happen in the TV series.

Believe me, it's all great fun and chock-full of stimulating talk and good information.

The best thing is that if The WB ever thinks about taking *Felicity* off the air, you'll see it there first—and you'll be able to help organize a write-in campaign to tell the people how much you love the show!

You can also write the stars or creators of *Felicity* at:

Felicity
The Warner Brothers Television Network
4000 Warner Blvd.
Burbank, CA 91522

NINETEEN

Show by Show

EPISODE #1

"Graduation" (the pilot)
Airdate: 9/29/98
Written by J. J. Abrams and Matt Reeves
Directed by Matt Reeves

After graduation ceremonies, Felicity Porter
steels her nerves in order to request a signature in
her high-school yearbook from a boy she's admired
from afar for four years, Ben Covington. Ben's
long entry makes Felicity regret she'd not spoken
to him before. When she discovers that Ben is going to the University of New York, Felicity fol-
lows.

In Manhattan, she discovers that Ben really isn't
interested in her, but they agree to be friends. She

makes friends with Ben's love interest, Julie—who breaks it off with Ben. When Felicity considers going back home, Noel, her resident dorm adviser, suggests that she stick it out, admitting he has feelings for her.

Despite her parents' displeasure, Felicity decides to stay.

EPISODE #2

"The Last Stand"
Airdate: 10/6/98
Written by J. J. Abrams
Directed by Matt Reeves

When Felicity discovers that someone has applied to read her admission essay to the University of New York, she thinks it's Ben and wonders if he has become interested in her. However, she quickly learns that it was her father who made the request when she visits her academic counselor and discovers her parents there—still in New York City. They still can't understand why she wants to stay at the Manhattan school and not attend Stanford.

They are horrified when Felicity tells them the truth about why she came to the University of New York. Things get straightened out when Noel speaks to Mr. Porter. Mr. and Mrs. Porter still aren't happy, but they realize that it's Felicity's decision to make and they respect her bravery and independence.

EPISODE #3

"Hot Objects"
Airdate: 10/13/98
Written by J. J. Abrams
Directed by Brad Siberling

Julie tells Felicity that she and Ben are through and that Felicity should ask him to a dorm party if she wants to.

Felicity sticks with premed and is excited about her inorganic-chemistry professor, who's the author of her high-school chemistry textbooks. Unfortunately, when Felicity is unable to obtain the class textbook, she earns the scorn of the professor.

In Ben's drama class, he is forced to show feeling concerning a "hot object"—something of importance to him.

At a party one of the tapes Felicity has made for her French tutor, Sally, gets mixed up with the music tapes. Everyone at the party hears Felicity talking about wanting to get physical with a man.

Ben gets locked out of his room and asks to sleep in Felicity's. They seem to be becoming better friends.

EPISODE #4

"Boggled"
Airdate: 10/20/98
Written by Mimi Schmir and J. J. Abrams
Directed by Todd Holland

In the laundry room, Felicity straightens out a misunderstanding with Julie, and they meet a funny film student named Zach.

While playing Boggle with Felicity, Noel gives in to an impulse to kiss Felicity. They are interrupted by Megan and Noel scrambles off in embarrassment.

In chemistry class, Felicity gets Elena, a dorm mate, for a lab partner. However, when Megan tells Elena that Felicity and Noel are having an affair, Elena believes this is why Felicity has managed to get a compact refrigerator for her room.

During a "maybe date," Noel tells Felicity that he has a girlfriend at another college. Felicity is angry.

Julie clumsily criticizes Zach's movie and he is hurt.

EPISODE #5

"Spooked"
Airdate: 10/27/98
Written by Jennifer Levin
Directed by Joan Tewkesbury

Felicity and Ben walk into a burglary in progress, and are mugged.

Felicity believes that Ben is getting closer to her when he arrives two nights in a row at her room to talk over the frightening experience.

Ben invites Felicity to a Halloween party, but then kisses a woman dressed as the Pink Power Ranger.

Outside the party, Julie freaks when Zach kisses her. Later she kisses him and they decide to just relax and see what happens.

Felicity, sick from the party punch, allows Noel to comfort her. But then she throws up on him.

EPISODE #6

"Cheating"
Airdate: 11/3/98
Written by Ed Redlich
Directed by Marc Buckland

While spell-checking an English-class essay for Ben, Felicity impulsively rewrites it to make it better.

When the professor suspects that Ben did not really write the paper, he starts an investigation that may get Ben expelled.

Meanwhile, Zach invites Julie to see a cult film called *Solaris*.

Blair wants to keep seeing Elena—but Elena keeps on breaking dates.

When Ben admits that he did not write the paper, Felicity confesses to save him. The English professor does not have them expelled, but they both fail the paper as punishment.

Ben is upset with Felicity.

EPISODE #7

"Drawing the Line, Part One"
Airdate: 11/10/98
Written by J. J. Abrams
Directed by Ellen Pressman
First of two parts.

After Blair thinks that Elena is having problems and she says she might be moving to another college, he sees her going into the financial-aid office. When Felicity uses her job in the student-affairs office to discover that Elena has lost financial support, she helps Blair find Elena a suitable scholarship.

Ben is not speaking to Felicity. Fellow dorm advisers urge Noel to "draw the line" regarding Felicity's need to talk to him about Ben. However, Ben realizes that Felicity only means well when he finds out about her help for Blair and Elena.

Zach has sex with Julie without her total consent.

EPISODE #8

"Drawing the Line, Part Two"
Airdate: 11/17/98
Directed by Joan Tewkesbury
Written by J. J. Abrams and Riley Weston

Felicity, Ben, Noel, Elena, and Blair rally to support their traumatized friend Julie.

Zach insists he did not rape her.

An angry Ben confronts Zach about Julie.

twenty

Music

From the moment its pilot episode was televised, music has played a vital part in creating the feeling of *Felicity*.

Felicity is all about moods and feelings, hopes and dreams, atmosphere and style, and working to becoming your best, truest self. That's why the lyrics are important to the songs used on the show.

The show's "background music" is done by W. G. "Snuffy" Walden.

The theme song was written by Larry Klein and J. J. Abrams.

Here's a list of songs from the show:

Show 1. "Graduation" (the pilot)

ARTIST: Madonna

SONG: "The Power of Goodbye"
ALBUM: *Ray of Light*

ARTIST: Ivy
SONG: "I've Got a Feeling"
ALBUM: *Apartment Life*

ARTIST: Sarah McLachlan
SONG: "Angel"
ALBUM: *Surfacing*

Show 2. "The Last Stand"

ARTIST: Jude
SONG: "Charlie Song"
ALBUM: *No One Is Really Beautiful*

ARTIST: Donny Hathaway
SONG: "Everything Is Everything"
ALBUM: *Everything Is Everything*

ARTIST: Neil Finn
SONG: "She Will Have Her Way"
ALBUM: *Try Whistling This*

ARTIST: Sarah McLachlan
SONG: "Good Enough"
ALBUM: *The Freedom Sessions*

ARTIST: Heather Nova
SONG: "Valley of Sound"
ALBUM: *Siren*

Show 3. "Hot Objects"

ARTIST: Coolio
SONG: "Oh La La"
ALBUM: *My Soul*

ARTIST: Drip Tank
SONG: "Mad at Me"
ALBUM: *Drip Tank*

ARTIST: Barry Adamson
SONG: "Something Wicked This Way Comes"
ALBUM: *Lost Highway Soundtrack*

Show 4. "Boggled"

ARTIST: Peter Gabriel
SONG: "Here Comes the Flood"
ALBUM: *Sixteen Gold Greats*

ARTIST: Mazzy Star
SONG: "So Tonight I Might See"
ALBUM: *Fade into You*

Show 5. "Spooked"

ARTIST: Liz Phair
SONG: "Baby Got Going"
ALBUM: *White Chocolate Space Egg*

ARTIST: Esthero
ALBUM: *Breath from An/other*

ARTIST: Money Mark
SONG: "Push the Button"
ALBUM: *Push the Button*

ARTIST: Marc Cohn
SONG: "True Companion"
ALBUM: *Marc Cohn*

Show 6: "Cheating"

ARTIST: Eagle Eye Cherry
SONG: "Save Tonight"
ALBUM: *Desireless*

ARTIST: Heather Nova
SONG: "Head and Shoulders"
ALBUM: *Siren*

ARTIST: Alpha
ALBUM: *Come from Heaven*

ARTIST: R.E.M.
SONG: "Drive"
ALBUM: *Automatic for the People*

Show 7: "Drawing the Line, Part One"

ARTIST: Ben Webster
SONG: "The Warm Moods"
ALBUM: *The Warm Moods*

ARTIST: Beck
SONG: "Tropicalia"
ALBUM: *Mutations*

ARTIST: The Getaway People
SONG: "She Gave Me Love"
ALBUM: *The Getaway People*

Show 8: "Drawing the Line, Part Two"

ARTIST: Jewel
SONG: "Absence of Fear"
ALBUM: *Spirit*

ARTIST: Family Stand
ALBUM: *Connected*

ARTIST: Kate Bush
SONG: "This Woman's Work"
ALBUM: *Sensual World*

Recently, on an *E! Online* chat, J. J. Abrams mentioned that Disney was busy making arrangements for the first *Felicity* CD Collection.

Can't wait!

twenty-one

Felicity Forever

"The last time I went to a club," Keri Russell told *TV Guide* in the November 7–13 "Young Hollywood" issue, "they would not let me in, and I almost cried. I'm gong to tell you what club it was because I want it to be in print: Jones."

Jones, in case you didn't know, is a hot and popular place in Hollywood where young stars sometimes like to hang out.

Well, true, Keri admits that she had her hair in a bun and wasn't wearing makeup or fancy clothes. Sounds like a *Felicity* moment, doesn't it?

However, I bet they'd let Keri in now!

Felicity is hot.

Not only was Keri on the cover of that *TV Guide*—but later on that week *Felicity* was lampooned on both *Mad TV* and *Saturday Night Live*—the same night!

And *People* magazine wanted to know who Keri thought was the "Sexiest Man Alive." (Keri didn't think there was just one, but she liked Paul Rudd and Michael Vartan, not just for their pizzazz but because "they look like they've read a book before in their lives.")

What's *Felicity*'s secret?

Besides dealing with important issues in fresh ways, I think that the show is so good because it does TV in a different way.

Each show, Matt Reeves and J. J. Abrams say, is like a little movie. And they aren't kidding. The sound, the lighting, the music, the editing, the acting—everything is carefully considered. This must take extra time and money, but somehow, in the pressure cooker of TV production, these guys pull it off.

Critics who've been checking in on the show's progress still like it. For instance, Marvin Kitman on *CNN Interactive* declares, "*Felicity* is the best drama of the year, a quality show of substance and intelligence, something worth watching."

Let's hope we all can keep on watching for a long time as the show grows and develops.

And maybe we'll be able to see Felicity go somewhere even more exciting than New York for grad school!

twenty-two

Felicity and College— True or False?

Felicity is a student at the "University of New York," a fictional college that sounds suspiciously like New York University, that artsy, angst-intense university in lower Manhattan. (Like Felicity's college, in New York film students are everywhere). But is Felicity having the genuine college experience?

We ran Felicity's experience by our panel of experts and they had a few comments to make.

TRUE OR FALSE?

◘ *It's easy to switch colleges at the last minute, as Felicity does?*

False! Why is Felicity in New York in the first place? Because at her high-school graduation she suddenly decided to follow Ben to New York City. But in real life, almost every university has filled all its places long before high-school graduation. In real life, if Felicity tried to follow Ben to New York, she'd be waiting tables and living in a sixth-story walk-up, and maybe applying to college for the next year. But would Ben go for a waitress? Even if he got free coffee?

¤ *Freshmen get big dorm rooms?*

Triple false! Being the low students on the totem pole, freshmen get the most cramped housing—especially in New York, where it's so crowded that even yuppies have to live in the hallways of other yuppies' apartments. A room the size of Felicity's would have at least four people in it. And someone who applied at the last minute, like Felicity, would probably be living in a rooming house in the far reaches of Brooklyn. And Felicity has the double luck that her roommate is always out—so she's conveniently alone when Ben needs a bed for the night. Poverty-stricken New York students would commit serious crimes for that kind of privacy!

¤ *College professors are like high-school teachers?*

False! In the show, Felicity's chem professor waits till the class is over then sits and eats lunch in his room. Hello? Didn't the director go to college? The professor could never sit down and dig out his sandwich, because professors move between classrooms. As soon as the chem students leave, a new group of students and professor will come streaming in. So where's a guy supposed to eat his sandwich? That's what offices are for.

¤ *Professors are called "Mister"?*

False! Here's another sign that the writers forgot lots about college. College professors pay $50,000 or so for that doctorate, and for $50,000, you'd insist on being called "Doctor," too. The ones who are still working for their doctorate usually insist on "Professor." If they knew Felicity and Ben were referring to them as "Mister," they'd get cranky faster than you could say "Mad Professor."

¤ *If someone else helps you write your paper, you'll be in big trouble?*

True *and* False! It's true that professors try to sniff out people who've copied their papers straight from library books, and getting someone else to actually write your paper is a serious academic crime. But in college, students are often encouraged to get help from their friends and other students who work as tutors, as long as you don't plagiarize someone else's work.

In *Felicity,* the prof suspects Ben's had help because his paper was good but he was flaky in class. If profs started condemning people because they're flaky in class, well, they'd be suspecting most of the student population. And truth to tell, professors don't want to start accusing students unless they've got proof a lot more solid than that. These days, when students feel they're mistreated, they sue. There's nothing a university wants to avoid more than a lawsuit.

¤ *People eat breakfast in college?*

False! Felicity and Julie seem to meet every morning in the cafeteria for a hearty breakfast and a discussion of the day's problems. Don't those problems involve staying up late? All-nighters are the very staple of college life—either for writing last-minute papers or for last-minute romance. . . . but mostly for movies and TV. Felicity won't really cut loose until she's pulling an all-nighter now and then—and until we don't see her at breakfast.

However, the professorial panel finds much in *Felicity* that is authentic . . .

¤ *College is supposed to be about academics, but actually everyone spends their time being obsessed with the opposite sex?*

True! You've got hundreds of attractive, pulse-pounding, hormone-emitting single people in the full flush of youth, thrown together every day, out of the reach of parents, with lots of time on their hands. They're doing calculus? Not on your life.

¤ *Watching weird movies is the big entertainment in college?*

True! Julie is right on the money when she worries that Zach will expect her to have an opinion about *Solaris,* the four-hour Soviet film about a space station. College is the real-world version of the Independent Film Channel, especially if you hang around film buffs like Zach. Good response for question about a film: "Intense." Bad response: "Doesn't anybody watch Beavis and Butt-head around here?"

¤ *Roommates are weird?*

This is the oldest fact in history. So, so true.

¤ *The people who oversee dorms are too responsible for their own good?*

True! Like Noel. He runs a great dorm. He's there every time there's trouble. Great for the dorm. But how's his private life? Unbutton a little, Noel!

So how does *Felicity* rate?

Overall, our profs give it a B-plus—"some good points, but could try harder!"

But we'd like to observe that the first semester is always a little rocky—give the show some time, and it could make the dean's list!